THAT'S THE WAY I LOVED YOU

CARRIE AARONS

Editing done by Proofing Style.

Cover designed by Okay Creations.

Thank you to way-back-when Taylor Swift for helping me write this book.
Your first and second albums were the soundtrack to Jason and Savannah.

Do you want your **FREE** Carrie Aarons eBook?

All you have to do is **sign up for my newsletter**, and you'll immediately receive your free book!

1

SAVANNAH

My cherry red nails click absent-mindedly on the table, a nervous tic I've never been able to cure manifesting in the anxious silence.

Perry lays a hand over mine, and my eyes shoot up to his dark brown ones. There is a slight hint of annoyance in them, that I can't sit still and instead have been drumming like a child, and I instantly feel the slight burn of shame at the back of my neck. This initial impression is everything, and my too-bold nail polish choice could be screwing it up for us.

"Everything all right?" Perry's voice is faux cheerful, with an edge of power as he directs his question to the loan agent.

Armand, the loan agent assigned to our case, taps on his keyboard, his face concentrated on the laptop in front of him. "Just double-checking something."

Those words gnaw at the lining of my stomach because double-checking doesn't sound like a good thing. We should be golden, set to go, in the clear for buying the penthouse we've been eyeing for months.

I feel Perry's hand tighten on fingers that he's keeping from drumming nervously on the cool marble table. We sit on one side, a unit in color-coordinating power suits. And on the other, it's a firing squad of the Upper East Side's most judgmental. There is Armand, flanked by two other agents from the mortgage company who hold equally unreadable stares as they assess us. Then there is the shrewd, forty-something woman who runs the board of the Pavel, the uber-elite building we're trying to move into. And finally, next to her, is the leasing agent for the penthouse we've been fighting for since it went on the market a little over sixty days ago.

My boobs are sweating under the lilac Chanel blazer Perry gave me as a Christmas present last year. The color doesn't do much for me, with my strawberry blond hair it's far too light and washes me out. But it's a designer label, and I know it makes Perry happy when I wear it. So I did.

After being together for four years, he's finally given in and agreed that we should move in together. Because Perry is almost eight years older than I am, and a perpetual bachelor, he's been reluctant to give up his solitary space. In the beginning, we had to move past a lot of obstacles. Our age difference, the way we'd been brought up, his often quiet brooding. But it was the softer side of him that hooked me, the one that would bring chicken soup to my apartment when I was sick. Or show up at one of my shooting locations with roses just because. He had been there for me in a very dark time before I became the woman I am today.

And I just can't wait to start this next chapter of our lives together.

"So, I'm seeing some inconsistencies in your credit score and the properties you reported to us, Ms. Reese," Armand says, an eagle eye skewering me to my chair.

My heart starts to beat wildly. Even after almost ten years of living in New York, I'm still not used to the way people direct questions at you. As if they have a hidden agenda, like the politeness they layer over skepticism is misleading enough not to ruffle your feathers.

Where I grew up, people just said what they thought. Everyone was genuine, and if something needed addressing, it was addressed. No skirting around things with flowery language and unreadable social cues.

I try not to shift in my seat. "I'm not sure what you're referring to. I rent my apartment, have never owned a property, and I only have the one credit card. There is no debt to my name."

Truthfully, there isn't. I'm a simpleton when it comes to money, something that frustrates Perry. I believe in paying all of my bills on time, which means two days early. I don't let him diversify my portfolio, and I won't put a cent into the stock market. With one checking and one savings account, plus a retirement fund, that's all I need to survive.

"While searching your social security number, there is a property listed. Number three Covered Wagon Lane?"

My heart plummets. I'd be surprised if I looked down and didn't see a hole in the floor, followed by a fallout of the sixteen floors below us. I swear, I almost double over and puke right there on the gleaming hardwood floors of the Pavel's conference room.

It's been almost a decade since I heard that address said out loud. Even longer since I've allowed myself to even think of it. But the moment Armand utters the words, that tiny cabin with the rusty red front door pops into my mind. And sadness, like a black sheath of mourning, clouds over my heart in anticipation of hurricane like storms.

"The property is in collections. Seems to have a few liens on it, and it looks like there is some interest of forecloseure on it." Armand scans over the screen and then flits his eyes back up to me.

Every eye in the room is trained on me, some expectant,

others smug, and more than one has a glimmer of disgust in it. These people are not used to the words collections and foreclosure.

Foreclosure. There is no way any bank one hundred square miles around Hale, Texas, would give a rat's ass about that junky shack in the woods. But how the hell is that property still even tied to me?

Because you left your hometown and never bothered to look back, a self-satisfied voice whispers in my ear.

I rub at my chest, not caring anymore if these people see a crack in the armor. Age-old wounds, ones I've merely stitched up haphazardly and ignored, open like it's ten years ago all over again.

How the hell did *he* not take care of this? The one thing left in his responsibility, and of course, he couldn't even manage to clean that mess up.

Chancing a glance at my Wall Street-trader boyfriend, I try my hardest to bite back the sheepish smile trying to form on my lips. Perry DeLeon is one of the smartest, most successful men I've ever met. He's gorgeous in that obvious way, with angular features and neatly trimmed brown hair. He looks just as good in a three-piece tux as he does in tennis gear, and for some reason, he picked me. When we met, I was a bumbling, mousy girl who still barely knew her way around the subway system. Perry seemed smitten from the moment we met, maybe because I seemed mysterious? In reality, I was trying not to choke on my tongue as I looked at him in his midnight black town car. He was like Mr. Big, driving up in a chariot to teach me the ways of New York City.

With him, I've transformed. I've traveled, I landed my dream job; we fell in love, and created a life that I only ever read about in storybooks.

I knew, at some point, my past would rear its ugly head. I've shoved it down, tried to tie bricks to its ankles and drown the girl I used to be. I never thought it would come to bite me in the ass, at least not this terribly.

Perry knows nothing of who I was before I landed face-first on the sidewalks of the city.

But I have a feeling that my wild, country roots are about to wind their way around us both, exposing the truths I've kept buried for far too long.

2

JASON

Midland sings on about having drinking problems as I slam another nail down into the roof.

My hand throbs, the calluses whining along with the chorus of a country song as I abuse the appendage. I've been at this for far too long, but pain is second nature in my life and I push past it.

"Jay, come on down. Quitting time!" Beau yells, and again, I ignore him.

The rest of the guys went home an hour ago, but I'm in a particularly shit mood, so I stayed up here. Not that I'm getting paid much, if anything, to be here. Beau should thank me for finishing this roof his guys have been working half-ass on their entire eight-hour shift. Because of me, they'll be able to start insulation tomorrow, and Beau will be that much closer to handing over the keys to this mansion to his hoity-toity clients.

I bring the hammer down, smacking a nail into its place, as I hear Beau start up his car.

"Don't get yourself killed," my best friend instructs out the driver's side window, before pulling away.

At least he knows what I need, even if I'm unwilling to say it.

I need to be alone, with country music drowning out my thoughts, and a hammer thwacking against a hard surface. Something my fists are not allowed to do, hence why I'm not down at Buddy's, the local bar. If I went there tonight, I'd end up in the sheriff's drunk tank.

I'm not sure why some days are harder than others. Maybe it's the change in the seasons, with the cool winter weather turning to spring. Maybe I didn't get enough sleep. Or maybe it's nearing closer and closer to that date on the calendar, the one I dread with each passing year.

Whatever it is, it's got me wound tighter than a spring-loaded coil, and the only thing that helps is working for free to pass the time between sun up and sun down.

My existence over the past ten years has become a restrained contentment. At the beginning, when I lost the two biggest dreams in my life, I drank myself into a stupor each day. It wasn't until I almost killed myself and another on the road through town, which resulted in a DUI and some heavy community service, that I started to clean it up.

After that, I bought my business, built it up, and run that thing like a well-oil machined in the months that it's viable. When I can't do that, I work on Beau's crew for fun, and because I can't just sit still. Sitting leads to thinking, which leads to sorrow, which leads to drinking, and well, I saw how that chapter ended.

Aside from work, I have my friends. Most folks in town know me, and my calendar is never empty of social events or community work I can do.

But it's the nights that spook me. That crawl their way under my skin and slice open the barely healed scars on my heart.

I hear the purr of the engine before I see it. Jesus, that driver has to be going over eighty, which is not only stupid on these winding roads but also illegal. And then it comes into view, the sleek gray BMW with the sunset glinting off of its body. From my position on the roof, I watch as it jets past, going faster than a bull just released from its gate at the rodeo.

"Jesus," I mutter to no one but myself.

Out-of-towners are the fucking worst. Whoever is in there is probably wearing designer labels, just passing through on their way to Dallas or Austin. No regard for our sleepy town and the residents who try to stay safe inside it.

Just as I'm about to turn back to my aggressive construction work, I hear sirens.

Lazily, I turn back around, feeling a smug sort of satisfaction when I see a pickup with the word sheriff emblazoned across it pulling out onto the road, in pursuit of the BMW.

Well, I guess I was wrong in my drunk tank assumption. Turns out, the sheriff isn't patrolling the local bar, but sitting out here in a speed trap. Sheriff Kevin Jenkins and I went to high school together, played ball, and now we have a standing poker night once a month with a couple other buddies.

He gets on her bumper, signaling for the driver to pull over, and he or she does. Prick is probably pissed off that a snoozing cop on a country road flagged him down. As Jenks walks to the car, I can see his authoritative gait and I have to chuckle. I've seen this guy drunk seven ways to Sunday, pissing on a field goal post at the high school, and now he's the law around here.

Good, I think when he reaches the car, *give 'em a whopper of a ticket*. Then, to my surprise, the driver opens the door to get out, and jumps into his arms. Jenks laughs as he sets the driver, a woman, down, and then I catch a glimpse of her hair in the setting sun.

I swear, I almost fall off of the roof.

Because I would notice that hair anywhere. Strawberry blond, the color of sunflowers as a blood-red sun descends down over them. The color of her mama's sweet banana and strawberry pie, which I can practically taste in my mouth right now.

That hair, the locks I've run my fingers through a thousand times ...

To say I'm baffled is an understatement. My eyes must be playing tricks on me. There is no way Savannah Reese is in Hale. She left ten years ago and never came back.

But I would swear, she's standing not a hundred feet from me. Thankfully, from my position on the roof, neither her nor the sheriff has noticed me.

They talk a little longer, and then she gets back in her car and drives off.

I watch that BMW until I can't see it any longer, but I know where it's headed. And when she takes the turn for the long road that leads to the lake, I'm sure of it.

Before I can think about what I'm doing, I'm scaling down from the roof and sprinting to my truck.

3

SAVANNAH

Gravel kicks up under the tires of the BMW coupe as I wind it around the trees, the headlights barely making the road visible.

If you can even call this a road. It's more of a path in the middle of the woods, and time has done it no favors. Back when I lived here, you could barely make it out even then. With all the weeds and brush cluttering it now, I can tell no one has been out here in years.

I come to a clearing, and squinting against the pure darkness of rural Texas, make out a small house in front of my headlights.

This place used to be my sanctuary. It was my dream home, once upon a time. This shanty, nothing more than a two-room hut fifty feet from the lake and secluded from the world ... it was paradise. God, how naive the Savannah I was back then had been.

Anyone else who had lived in New York City for the last ten years would be scared to get out of the car. But not me. These were my boondocks, the ones I'd run wild in under the starlight since I could sneak out of my bedroom window at the age of ten. Those native NYCers were probably more likely to be murdered at their favorite Chinese restaurant around the block, yet the woods at night are what they're afraid of.

Stepping from the car, I'm glad I opted for my flat knee-high boots instead of the spike-heeled black ones I'd thrown in my bag. Because as soon as my foot makes contact with the ground, it's met with a mud that only wet season in Texas could provide.

The house is in worse shape than it was the day we bought it. I can see a missing section of the tin roof, the one we used to lie under and listen to the thunder clapping down on. The windows are grimy and fogged, and I'm pretty sure they're not keeping any kind of cool air out of the inside of the structure. The front door hangs off-center, and I'm pretty sure I'll break my neck if I step foot on the front porch.

There was a moment in time when I pictured being carried across the threshold as a married woman; carrying our first baby through it. I'd dreamed of a bright red door, something like the shade of my nails, and blue-trimmed windows. I'd had my eye on two rocking chairs; the handmade kind two nineteen-year-olds never could have afforded.

And then my whole life went sideways, and it all collapsed, just like this old shack.

"She's still a beaut, ain't she?"

The voice comes out of the shadows, startling me and sending my heart clattering against my ribcage. I don't jump though, because I know it. I'd know it anywhere. Even though I've forbidden myself from hearing it in memories or thinking about it during the waking hours, I can't help the dreams that always come in sleep.

Deep, deeper than it was the day I left at nineteen, with a twang only his roots could provide. It's got a hint of grizzly husk to it, and I bet if that voice whispered in my ear, it could still do that tingling, electric thing to my spine.

"Not exactly the word I'd use." I don't turn, my hands

shaking at the thought of my eyes holding him in them for the first time in a decade.

"Well, one man's trash is another man's treasure. Or does it all just look like trash coming from the big city?" He almost snorts, the snideness in his tone making me want to slap him.

It could have been ten years or ten seconds, but I'd never get over the feelings Jason Whitney gave me. From the first moment I met him, all the way back at the church bake sale when I was eight, I'd been in love with him.

We were ... on fire. Blazing hot every damn minute of our existence with each other, whether it was burning with love or scorching with hate. Well, that's a different story. Everyone knew not to come close to Savannah and Jason when we were in a fight. But not five minutes later, he'd be hauling me up into that truck and doing things that would make everyone in town blush if they were witness.

It shouldn't be a surprise that he's out here, even though the question is on the tip of my tongue. Someone in town must have heard, or Sheriff Jenkins—how weird it was to say that—told him. Or maybe he simply knew; we always did have the kind of connection that was cosmic, something even the stars couldn't explain.

Finally, I turn, and even if he's half-shadowed by the woods, the image still makes my heart go from a gallop to a sprint.

Moonlight falls over that raven hair, the shade so close to the midnight sky that I used to tease him he'd come from a crow ancestry. He's bigger now, if that's even possible. I was always so petite compared to Jason, but the person standing before me isn't the high school boyfriend who would catch me around my waist in the middle of the hall.

No, this is a man. A strapping, muscled, filled out in all the right areas ... *man*. He's rugged in a way that no man in the city, especially Perry, will ever be. Just being in his proximity turns me on, and that pisses me off even more. I should have more control, I've had ten years to get this reaction under control.

I can only make out one eye that's illuminated by the moonlight, but that's enough. So blue that it's more iridescent than the middle of a sapphire, that eye, and its twin, used to hypnotize me. Those light blue orbs held every secret of mine and all the words that can't be said right now.

As Jason nears me, the force field of tension around us growing stronger with each step, I notice the stutter. The way his left leg drags behind just a second longer. Every inch of me fills with paralyzing sadness. His limp, unnoticeable to any stranger, is a physical reminder of all we've lost. To the untrained eye, they wouldn't even catch the lag. But they haven't seen him run, haven't seen his body stretch to the most unimaginable athletic feats possible.

"What're you doing here, Savvy?" He uses the nickname I ditched the second I crossed the Texas state border a decade ago.

Him, saying that, it brings it all flooding back. The love, the hurt, the horrible, soul-crushing breakup. And that ... that makes me furious. He has no right to question me, to throw wrenches in my life and make me return to Hale.

My voice is venom when I speak.

"Wondering how the hell you sunk this piece of shit even farther into the mud. And how I can dig us out of it so I can go back home to my life, my boyfriend, and my new apartment."

4

JASON

Getting hit by a tractor trailer would have hurt less.

Not only did she just emphasize that Hale was no longer her home—a fact I've known for some time but refused to get on board with—but she threw in that line about the boyfriend simply to gut me.

Savannah has a boyfriend. And by the way it sounds, one she is moving in with.

I don't think my heart could be mashed into ground beef any more than it already is. Seriously, someone fry it up on a griddle and just eat it, put me out of my misery.

I'm not sure why I thought she'd be there, pining for me in the same way I did for her. The Savannah in my brain was the exact same girl who had left ten years ago, yet the woman standing in front of me was anything but that.

She seemed taller, though for Savvy, tall was never the word anyone would use to describe her. She was barely five foot two, back in the day, so maybe it was those fancy boots doing the trick. Those boots looked like they cost more than my whole house, which was my first clue as to how much she'd changed.

The BMW, the dress pants and blouse she wore under a

long, soft brown trench coat. The boots, the way her hair, still its same color, looked tamed and bright. Gone were the days of her locks snarled with leaves and ragged from running around in the creek beds with me.

Or maybe it's just the air about her. There is a way people who live in this town hold themselves; in a genuine, true manner. We're open, willing to lend a hand or an ear depending on the situation. But with people who don't grow up in small towns ... you can just tell how detached they are. Everything about their body language screams, "keep your distance."

That's exactly what Savannah was saying now, without saying it.

She's still every bit as gorgeous. Every bit as striking as the day I'd first kissed her in the eighth grade. But it couldn't be denied, a bit of her spark had burned out.

"You can fix it up if you'd like, darlin'. Got some tools in the truck." I jack a thumb toward my pickup, ignoring her second statement about the debt.

"How does that thing even still run?" Savannah looks part amused, part disgusted.

Is she thinking about all the times I laid her down in the bed of my truck? Because now that she's looking at it, I sure am.

"When you take the time and effort to keep fixing something, it won't give up on you." My words are ominous.

"Don't talk to me about giving up on something." Savvy's words are equally as haunting.

We're in a standoff, staring at each other on the land that used to be our saving grace.

We'd bought the little shack house from my uncle, the only family I'd had back then, the day I turned eighteen. He was willing to part with it for the sweet tune of three thousand dollars, but it was the land that was worth anything. Really, I think he just wanted me out of the house. He co-signed a loan for us at the bank, and I set to work that day on making it the home that Savannah had always dreamed of.

It's nothing more than a large living space with a tiny kitchenette and barely closed-off bathroom, with an adjoining bedroom that could *just* fit a queen bed and dresser.

We'd moved in the day after high school graduation, after I'd laid the last new floorboard and painted the bedroom a canary yellow that she'd picked out. Everyone said we were crazy, and hell, we were. Crazy in love, about each other, and just about every other shade of crazy under the sun.

But we were determined to make it. I had a dream that could earn us more dollars than we'd ever seen, and Savannah came along for the ride. Until it ended, killing all of my hopes. Then the unimaginable happened, just one whopping tragedy on top of another.

Apparently, we weren't strong enough to weather the storm.

"How the hell could you let this property lapse? Why the hell didn't you sell, back then?" Her voice is incredulous, and flames lick at the edges of her eyes.

I've always loved her fury. "Seems there were two of us who owned it. You can't put the blame squarely on me."

That answer only serves to irritate her further, and I swear she stamps a boot-clad foot in the dirt. "I left, Jason. That gave you clear ownership, in my mind, to sell the damn place. You could have made a pretty penny off this land. Instead, my loan agent back in New York tells me you haven't paid the mortgage on the land or the property taxes in almost ten years! What the hell were you thinking?"

That you'd come back for it. For me, a small voice in my head whispers, but I shut it up.

"I was thinking that no one has any right to own land out here more than God himself, and that doing anything requiring a credit score is something I could just complete myself."

"That's some jackass, hillbilly kinda—" Savannah starts cursing under her breath, too angry to address me.

"I'll give you the money. Right now. I have my checkbook. You tell me what's owed on it, how we get off our bankrolls, and I'll write it out right now." She's so matter of fact that I want to kiss her square on the mouth.

Shock her. Send that professional, disinterested attitude running back to the city it came from.

But I don't. Instead, I turn around and head for my car. "I'm not selling it."

I can hear Savannah scrambling under her breath. "But ... what ... what do you mean you're not selling?"

"You heard me." I never do like to repeat myself, and she should remember that fact.

"Jason! Don't you dare get in that truck!" she hollers, that twang I love so much coming back in her anger.

I smile, though she can't see it as I'm turned away. Yell at me, fight. Anything to make you sound a little more like the girl I used to make fall apart on the mattress in that shack behind us.

"Why in the hell won't you just settle this? Haven't we hurt each other enough? Don't be spiteful, just to be spiteful!" she pleads.

She doesn't understand, though. If I handed this over, if I let her sign the check, she'd be cashing in my last card. The only one I have left to play.

The only thing I have still tying her to me.

5

SAVANNAH

"I know, Per, I'm trying."

The frustrated sigh that comes across the phone only grates on my nerves more. "They're only going to hold the sale for us for the next thirty days. After that, they'll give it to the next highest bidder."

As if telling me just how dire of a situation this is makes me feel any calmer. "At least they gave us an extension. I'm sure I can settle what I need to here, and then it'll all be fine. I really do apologize, again ... I don't know how this happened."

There is a silence on the other end, and I just picture him pinching the bridge of his nose, sitting behind his gleaming glass desk in a navy blue pinstripe suit.

"How did you never tell me about this, Savannah? It's just so ... irresponsible. I've never known you to be irresponsible." Perry's tone makes me cringe.

It's because, with him, I'm not irresponsible. I'm not the girl barely escaping run-ins with the local cops, or moving out at eighteen to live with her boyfriend. I'm not the girl who left her family, missing the only time she had left with—

Shaking my head to clear the cobwebs I haven't allowed to

settle in my brain for years, I cough. "I'm sorry, it's just my past. Something I thought was buried and done. I'll take care of it. I just can't wait to come home to you."

I try to infuse a small smile into my voice, because the thought of Perry and New York feels like home. And I'm so disjointed right now, from being back in Hale, from seeing Jason, that all I want is the comfort of my safe life miles and miles from here.

"I can't wait either." He sighs, sounding tired. "I miss you. Things here are just hectic and work is insane ... I need you back here. Okay?"

"I know." I have to swallow the emotion.

But before I can go on, telling him how much I love him, Perry cuts me off. "Ah, shit, something's just come through to my desk. I gotta go, Savannah. Talk later."

The line goes dead, and I notice how he never told me that he loved me. My parents never went a day without telling each other they were so in love. Multiple times a day, enough to make us kids fake gag on our fingers.

Walking back into the strange house I've come to stay in, I try not to wince at the hundreds of ceramic pigs and chickens littering the counters, top of the cabinets, and in the clear glass of the sideboard by the table.

After Jason left me standing in the dark, out in the middle of nowhere, last night, I could barely find the control to call my sister. Adeline, along with our other two siblings, still lives in Hale. She's married, with three kids, and was so shocked to hear from me that she all but dropped the phone. Which is still attached to the wall by one of those chords, as I witnessed when I walked into her home not more than an hour later.

Now, here I am, up before everyone else in the house to catch Perry in the three minutes he has to chat before the clock strikes seven a.m. on the East Coast. But here, in our sleepy

Texas hometown, the whole family is still snoozing comfortably in their beds at six on a weekday. Back home, I'd be in a spin class or on my way for a venti coffee at Starbucks by this time. I'd be on set before my sister and her children had even caught the school bus and be home far after the sun went down. I'd bet money on it that Adeline has dinner on the table at five, and they all eat together, discussing their day.

My, how different our lives have turned out.

At the counter, I find the coffee pot, a generic model that Perry would scoff at. The thought makes me cringe, because how much has the city, has he, influenced my mind? Back in the day, I wouldn't have even noticed. But as I pull the Folgers from the cabinet, the same place our mother left it when we were kids, I can't help but long for the dark, bold European brand that Perry stocks at his apartment.

Part of me loathes the kind of person I've become.

The pot brews, I pour a cup in a Hale High School Football mug and then sit at Adeline's kitchen table. Looking around, her overdone country rustic decor assaults my eyes. It's too much, everywhere, but I have to admit, it's somewhat comforting. No matter how far from Hale I've run, being back in its homey arms does feel nice.

"Well, this is different than Dad having to drag you by the feet out of your bed."

My sister rounds the table. I'm not sure how long I've been sitting here in silence, as she goes for the counter.

She's older, gray hairs popping up at the crown of her head, but still beautiful. Adeline was always the most graceful, the enviable older sister to us all. It went Adeline, Noah, Lorelei, and then me. The baby of the bunch, my siblings often taunted me, loved on me too hard, and complained that our parents allowed me to do things they'd have whipped the others' hides for. My brother and two sisters were presumably close, not that I'd know. I've barely spoken to them in ten years.

After ... everything happened, I took off. I cut ties, stopped answering the phone. I was terrified they blamed me. And maybe it was better with me gone, because it's not like any of them tried to chase me down.

In fact, I think this is the first time in a decade that Adeline and I have sat in the same room.

"Thanks for picking me up last night," I say, more into my coffee mug than to her.

"I thought it was a ghost calling. When I heard your voice, I dang near dropped the phone. Brad all but sat me down in a chair."

Her husband, Bradley, was still asleep upstairs somewhere. Adeline and Brad, Hale's forever couple. Together since middle school, they were married in the church on Main Street just after their twentieth birthdays. I barely stuck around for their honeymoon and missed each of my niece's or nephew's births.

When those kids come down the stairs, their faces will hold confused, unknowing looks. They have no idea who I am.

"I'll try to get a room at the inn, if there is one available. Don't worry, I won't be in your hair for long." Taking my cup to the sink, I rinse it out.

"No one said I was worried. You don't have to leave. Though I'd love to know the answer to the question of the hour. Why are you staying?" Ah, there is the big sister voice I've always hated.

My back is to her, and my guard is up. I don't want my business all over town, and I'm not sure if Adeline can be trusted anymore. My family and I are strangers, so will they really treat me as one of their own?

"Unfinished business. And then I'm back to New York."

Upstairs, a toilet flushes, and I hurry to grab my coat and

slide into my shoes. I'm not in the mood for a family reunion, and I already feel out of place here.

"That unfinished business wouldn't have to do with Jason, now would it?" She doesn't even bother to hide her smirk as I turn to face her.

"You don't know where I could find him on a morning like this, do you?" I ask, ignoring her.

She taps her chin. "Probably at The Whistlestop, or down at the school crosswalk. It's cold season."

I have no idea what that means, but I take it. I wanted to avoid going to Main Street, too many old memories, but I guess my ghost of Hale past has come calling.

"It is good to see you, ya know. It's been too long, Savvy." Adeline's eyes crinkle at the corners as she smiles a true, genuine smile at me.

I nod a fraction at her, acknowledging that it has been a long time.

And then I'm out the door, ready to find the ex-love of my life and wring his neck.

6

JASON

Steam blows burning hot onto my hand, and I mutter a loud curse that I'm certain was not under my breath.

One of the teenage customers waiting at the counter giggles, while old Mrs. Leftim scowls at me.

"Sorry," I say sheepishly as I pour two steaming hot espresso shots into the to-go cup in front of me.

"Burn yourself again?" Rudy, owner of The Whistlestop, chuckles at me from the register.

"The damn thing has a grudge against me." I flick off the espresso machine, much to the dismay of Mrs. Leftim.

I fill a couple more drink orders, seeming to quell the chaos that comes every ten minutes in these morning hours on Main Street.

I've never understood why he named this place The Whistlestop, as there are absolutely no trains that pass through Hale. Maybe it's because the place is so small, it reminds people of the cafes they have right next to the train station. Maybe it's just nostalgic, another thing to remind us we live in the smallest of towns.

Whatever it was, Rudy has owned the coffee shop for close to forty years. Well, he and his wife did, until she passed last spring. So, I agreed to come help him in the winter months, when his arthritis flairs up and he can't pull all the levers and fill all the pots. I also bought him one of those fancy espresso machines, because I was tired of the traitors driving twenty minutes to go get their lattes from name brand stores.

Now, there is a line of ten people out the door on this Tuesday morning, and when I spot a flash of strawberry blond hair among them, I have to grit my teeth.

Shit, who told her where I'd be?

"Savannah? Savannah Reese?" someone bellows, and I have to duck my head even farther.

Someone in the line has recognized her, and in a second, they'll all be turning their eyes to her. Then they'll turn their eyes to me, gauging my reaction as my high school sweetheart waltzes back into town.

See, this is what happens when you live in a town with a total of five stoplights. Everyone knows everyone else's business. These people either grew up with you, watched you grow up, or now has a kid who is growing up with your kid. Not that I have any kids to speak of; hell, at least I think.

"Smith? Holy hell, you haven't changed a bit!" Savannah exclaims, and from the corner of my eye, I see her embrace a large, hulk of a man near the front door of the shop.

There is a giggle or two from her, a few husky deep words from him, and then just as I suspect, I look up, and all eyes are on me.

"Oh, come on, people." I sigh, rolling my eyes, and everyone seems to snap back to pretending like they're not all staring between Savannah and me.

They all know the story of how we imploded. Just like they know how heartbroken and sullen I've been about love for the last ten years. So yeah, this is about to make front-page news on the Hale gossip wires.

"What brings you back to town, girl? I ain't seen you since we egged Mr. Edgars house just before graduation night." Smith rubs Savannah's back, and I want to rip his hand off with my teeth.

Smith always was kind of a jackass. He was in our grade all through school and hung around our group. But we weren't friends. He played football; I played baseball. He liked to take advantage of drunk girls when we had bonfires out on the lake shore, and I had always been a one-woman man. Plain and simple, Smith was an asshole. Still is. Parading around this town like he owns it or something because his daddy left the town's steel plant to him to manage.

"Oh my lord, that was a long time ago. Still funny, though." Savannah puts her tiny hand to her heart, as if she's trying to contain the hilarity.

Her accent is coming out in full force, even though she was all Yankee pride with me last night.

I'm making drinks, keeping my head down, when Rudy breathes a dreamy sigh next to me. "Well, if it isn't the prettiest girl to ever set foot in Texas herself."

"Oh, Rudy, stop it. I've missed you." She squeezes his hand. "Where's Loretta today?"

The whole place goes quiet at her mention of Rudy's late wife. And the minute the silence descends, I see panic set into Savannah's eyes. I want to be the one who puts the sadness there.

"She passed last year. Hell of a star this town lost." I give her a pointed look, as if to rub it in that she wasn't here.

A couple of *amen's* and *may her soul rest's* are spoken out from the dozen or so people drinking their morning coffee inside the shop.

"It was her time, darlin'. She sure would have been glad to see you back, though." Rudy gives Savannah a teary smile and pats the hand he's still holding.

"Rudy, I'm so ... so sorry. I didn't know."

"No, you didn't." I shoot at her from my place down the counter.

She doesn't know about a lot of things that have gone on here since she left. Savannah Reese thinks she can just waltz back into town, have her way with it, and leave again like a breeze on the wind. She has no regard for those she left behind, what has happened here since, or how much it will hurt to see her face and then never glimpse it again.

And someone ought to serve that dish to her cold.

Rudy gives me a sharp look, like he knows what I'm after and won't tolerate it. "Not your fault, sweetheart. Say, what can I get ya? We got one of those fancy espresso machines now, like your kind loves in New York."

She looks so uncomfortable, which serves her right. "Uh, I'll take a cappuccino, please."

When she pulls out her wallet, Smith interjects, "Please, let me."

She bats her eyelashes at him, and I want to deck the motherfucker. Or maybe haul her to my chest. I don't even know anymore. My emotions are so out of whack that I feel like I might explode at any moment.

"We need to talk," Savannah says, the moment she's in front of me and I'm making her drink.

I don't know why, but I'm being extra careful, making sure everything is measured in proportion for her cappuccino. *Jesus Christ, Jason, making her the perfect coffee won't convince her to stay in Hale.*

"How did you know where to find me? Been asking around?" I give her a shit-eating grin.

She looks like she's grinding down her back molars. "Cut the crap, Jason. We have business to hash out."

"It's all business with you. I think you forget what it's like to actually care about your neighbors as if they were your own family."

"Says the guy who is working as a barista. What, they didn't have a job for you down at the Piggly Wiggly?"

Of course, everyone in here is listening to our conversation, most of them not even bothering to look like they're not. Their looks are quizzical, because Savannah has made one huge error in my situation. But I hold up a hand, hoping that it cuts them all off from telling the truth.

"Actually, I tried pumping gas down on Highway 35, but they already had a full-time worker. So, espresso slinging it was." I shrug.

She thinks she knows me, thinks I'm still that washed up, useless piece of shit who couldn't get out of bed when his dream fell apart. Her opinion of me is so low, and why should I correct it? Loving someone isn't about how much money they make or if their career is one that kids strive for when they get into college. You love the person for their soul. And clearly, Savannah knew nothing about that anymore.

A frustrated huff passes her lips. "Can you just be serious for one damn minute? I really need to speak with you, Jason."

Hearing her say my name is like a bullet through the heart. "And I say, we don't have nothin' to talk about."

I swear, Savannah all but stamps her foot, then lowers her voice. "Let me just write you a check. You're really messing up a big thing for me."

"Seems I never can stop messing up when it comes to you," I say quietly, so no one else hears.

For a moment, we stare at each other, so many old memories coming to life between us.

"Come by and see some of your old friends at Buddy's tonight, and maybe we can have a chat then. Here's your coffee. Hope it's not to white trash for you."

The look she gives me could kill a thousand house plants.

But as much as I hate why she's here, I'll take any opportunity to see her. If I can get her under the same roof as me, I'm going to make it happen.

7

SAVANNAH

I can hear the honky-tonk music from inside my rented BMW.

The car smells like a long ago lit cigarette, which tells so much about the only car rental place at the Timula Airport, the one regional airport that gets you within an hour of Hale.

Flipping down the driver side visor, I check my teeth for lipstick in the mirror, and then pinch my cheeks twice. I've already applied a thin coat of makeup, nothing like the evening looks I'd put together in New York, sometimes with the help of hair and makeup artists. No, that was far too dramatic for this. Just a sweep of foundation, a swoosh of brown glittery eyeshadow, and a few coats of mascara. That and a nude lip, and I was good to go.

As it is, I'll be the best dressed person in here with dark blue skinny jeans and an emerald green puff-sleeve blouse. I'd switched my heels for chunky boots at the last minute, knowing that the grime of Buddy's floors didn't need to be anywhere near a good pair of Manolo's.

Plus, I didn't need Jason to think I'd gotten all dolled up for him. Not that my heart wasn't pounding in its chest, wondering what he saw when he looked at me now. Did he think I looked old? Was it still the same for him when our eyes met?

As much as I want to deny it, to banish the feeling, each time I drink him in, I'm transported right back to the street-lit nights and stolen kisses under the bleachers in gym class.

I've been dreading running into people, but here I am, walking into the lion's den. Not that being at The Whistlestop today was all that bad, aside from everyone in the place taking bets on how long it would take for Jason and me to run away together. Or rip each other's throats out. Either or.

No, going to Main Street this morning had actually been ... nice. Seeing Rudy, Smith, some of the girls I used to cheer with in high school, it was pleasantly comforting. I'd always had nightmares about coming back here, about people having that horrible sympathy in their eyes. But maybe it had just been too long. Since I'd been back, all of a day and a half, most of the old acquaintances I'd run into were just happy to see me.

And in most cases, I was too. Except for when I'd found out about Loretta's passing and realized I wasn't here. How many things had I missed while I'd been gone?

While in New York, I'd barely thought about home. All the painful, golden, lifetime's worth of memories were tightly locked in a box inside my brain that I never took out for fear of collapsing into my emotions. I'd forgotten how much I loved these people, and how much they loved me. I'd forgotten the buzz of a Friday night football game, when the whole town shut down, or church on Sunday mornings when Mama would cook pancakes for dozens of people.

The whine of a banjo in some song blaring from the speakers inside Buddy's breaks me from my reverie.

"Here goes nothing," I mumble as I climb out of the car and head toward the front door.

I'm hit with a blast of stale beer, cheap perfume, and a mess of an eighties country love song. I might not live in Texas anymore, but I do still listen to the genre, and this is the worst of it.

I'm scared to even inch my way inside, since the whole joint seems to be five beers deep and it's only nine p.m.

"Well, I'll be ..."

A familiar twang hits me in the right ear, and then a squeal comes at me as someone locks their arms around me.

"Sassy Savvy, they said you was back in town!"

I wriggle free of my captor and turn to see two big green eyes staring at me like an excited puppy dog. I'd recognize them anywhere, though it has been a very long time since I've seen them.

"Cecily!" I laugh, hugging her just as hard.

As we embrace, I wonder to myself if she's ticked off that I left. That I've never tried to keep in touch. I would be furious if my best friend dropped off the face of the earth and never bothered to call.

But that wasn't Ceci. She was never one to hold grudges or be anything but sweet as the tea her meemaw used to make us in the summer. We grew up together, Savvy and Ceci. Everyone in town knew we were inseparable, that is until Jason came into the picture. We were all thick as thieves, but he became my number one. Not that she minded. Cecily was so easy and kind that she'd show up when she was invited and find fun when she wasn't.

I've missed her, I realize, as I hold her now at an arm's length. "You haven't changed a bit."

"And you've changed a whole bucket! Gosh darn, girl, look at you! You look like something out of a magazine. So fancy!" She bounces on her heels, her lithe frame jittering like it always did.

Cecily is like a carbonated fairy, with her white-blond hair and elfish features, she looks like something out of *Peter Pan*. And never stops moving.

"Just a little New York glow up, I guess." I shrug, looking around. "You still live in town?"

She nods, motioning for the bartender and then picking up her own beer. "Of course, I'd never leave Hale. I love it too much. You remember Thomas?"

A tall, lean guy bends over the bar, catching Cecily's cheek with his lips. It's then that I notice the sparkle of a small engagement ring and band on her finger and the regular gold band on his hand that's pressed against the bar top.

"You're married?" I'm so shocked I can't speak.

There was a time where I assumed I'd be Cecily's maid of honor, and she'd be mine. We talked about raising babies together, attending their school events, and drinking wine on our porches on weekend nights. And I wasn't even invited to her wedding.

Thomas looks vaguely familiar; maybe he was a few years ahead of us in school. With the way he's looking at her, it's clear they're in love.

"Going on three years now. It wasn't anything fancy, nothing up to the New York standard, but we loved it. We live over on Church Street, got our own house and everything. And Buddy turned over management to Thomas last year." She waves her hand around the bar.

"Oh, well, that's ... great." I don't know how else to respond.

I'd all but forgotten about Cecily in the past ten years, a fact I'm not proud of now that the shame of it creeps up the back of my neck. Caught up in my own despair, heartbreak, and devastation, I'd erased all of Hale and its occupants from my mind. But here she is, happy and beautiful, and living the life she'd always imagined.

It made the little voice in the back of my head wonder if I was living the life I'd always imagined.

"So, are you married? Someone mentioned something about a boyfriend." Her smile is nothing but genuine.

In New York, almost all of my friends, or couple friends of Perry and mine, only asked questions to fish for information. But people like Cecily truly wanted to know if I was happy, I didn't even have to wonder about it.

I shake my head, noticing a couple other people listening in on our conversation. "Yes, I do. And no, we're um, we're not married. But we are going to buy an apartment together, this beautiful penthouse, so ..."

She nods enthusiastically, like it's all just so wonderful. She doesn't make some jealous expression at our grand apartment or judgmental face at the fact that we're not married. Because other people's business and accomplishments wasn't her business, she didn't covet it, and I just wasn't used to that anymore.

"Well, sure glad they don't let you drive around that city," Jenkins, who is now the sheriff, pipes up from down the bar. "You'd clear take someone's head off on all those crowded streets."

The fact that Jenks thinks you're not allowed to drive in the city shows just how much he doesn't know about living in New York. He's sitting next to Asher, Kyle, and Nicholas, three of Jason's old baseball buddies. Next to them are Breeland and Corey, a couple we used to hang out with in high school that married at the ripe old age of eighteen.

"You shush," I admonish him jokingly. "Hey, Thomas, can I buy a round for everyone in here?"

The bartender's eyes go wide, but I pull out my credit card and hand it to him. A couple of people hoot, some others give me a hawk eye, and Cecily is still right there, smiling. I'm not sure what Jason wants me to do here, or where the hell he is, but I'll show a gesture of goodwill.

"Did you hear that, folks? She thinks we can't buy our own beers."

I turn, knowing that sarcastic, biting tone anywhere. "Beau, it's good to see you."

Jason's best friend comes to settle at the bar next to me, looking me up and down. "Can't say I feel the same."

Ah, I get it. He's pissed off about how I left his best friend. I wonder if any of these people know the real story, considering I wasn't here to tell my side of the truth. Nah, after Jason got injured and my world went sideways, I took off, not bothering to tell anyone why.

"Pity, because you'd get a free beer out of it. Thomas, round for everyone but Beau." I give Jason's friend an evil grin.

Beau and Jason were like brothers, considering Jay pretty much grew up at Beau's house. When we started dating, he was all but adopted by my family, and slept nights at Beau's house. Jason had little to no family; his mama took off when he was born, and his daddy died overseas in a tank explosion when he was six. Technically, Jason should have been a ward of the state, but the town of Hale raised him like a village. With one lone uncle who drifted in and out of town every once in a while, so he could claim custodianship, and then the people who really loved him could provide for him. Beau's family, Rudy and Loretta, a couple of his baseball families ... they all pitched in and made sure he was fed, clothed, and thriving.

That was what Hale was like. And it isn't until right this second I miss it so intensely, that I feel an aching in my soul.

"It is good to see you, though, even if I'm the devil to you now. You look good, Beau." I pat his arm.

He shoots me a look with a bushy brown eyebrow. "I had to come down here tonight instead of tucking my daughters into bed to make sure you didn't break his heart again. What're you doing here, Sav?"

"You have kids?" I say in shock.

"We are thirty now. Or did you stop mentioning your age like you fancy women like to? I grew up," he mocks me.

My nose turns up. "I'm twenty-nine and holding onto every last day of it. How many kids do you have?"

But Beau sees through my tactic. "What are you doing here?"

Almost everyone in the bar is now ignoring us, and no one else has come up to greet me in happiness. I feel the sour looks from every corner; I'm the enemy here. For a town that once loved me, they took his side in our sort of divorce.

"She's trying to sell our house, that's what she's doing here. She's trying to cut her last tie with Hale."

Jason sidles up to us, and I'm so surprised by his quiet approach that I startle. He puts a hand to my back, since I almost knock into him and the two glasses full of beer that Thomas just set down in front of us, and it's the first time he's touched me in ...

Forever.

It feels like taking a drink after thirsting for a millennium. That light splay of his fingers is home. It's the massive puzzle piece-sized chunk that's been missing from my life for ten whole years.

I both hate that I crave it and lean into the completeness of it.

Jason and I, we were magnetic. Fate had decided on us for each other and wanted it to be so. For a very long time, I'd never questioned that. I'd taken it as fact.

But that was once upon a time. And this was after the fallout.

So I shrink away, back to my own personal bubble, and pretend his hand didn't linger there for longer than it needed.

8

JASON

Hours later, a tipsy Savannah follows me out to the parking lot.

"Seriously, Jason, you're not even going to talk about this? I showed up here tonight because you asked, and I thought you'd be mature and have a discussion. How little I forget."

She throws her hands up, and I can feel the white wine coming out of her pores from here. After her first beer, she switched to Chardonnay. When we were together, she couldn't stomach anything dryer than Moscato, but I guess New York really has changed her, palette and all.

She's only had three drinks, but even I can tell she's swaying too much to drive herself. I should go get Cecily, ask her to take Savannah back to wherever she's staying, but I'm a masochist. I love her anger, her annoyed tone. Because it means attention, and it's been so long since she's given me any.

Yep, I'll stab the knife into my own heart.

"Wasn't it nice to see your old friends?" I dig deeper, trying to get under her skin.

She nears me as I lean against the driver's door of my truck.

How many times have we been in this exact position, but with her between my legs, pressing her lips to mine? My fingers still spark from the contact I made with her back in there, almost two hours ago.

I hate that she's the only woman I will ever crave. I can't stand the thought of her being with another man. I want to rage against the world for having us end up this way.

"Yes." She touches a finger to her lip, ruminating on it. "It actually was."

Because she hadn't just given up on me. Savannah's entire life, all the people who loved her, had been here. Most of them still were. I was so fucking disappointed that she'd abandoned them. Hell, she hadn't even been on the radar to attend Cecily's wedding, and that was just tragic.

"See? I'm enriching you as a person. Making you a human again." My smile is sickeningly sarcastic.

"Pssh, because what? My morality has been ruined since I've been away? Get over yourself, Jason. The world is a bigger place than just Hale, Texas."

I lower my eyes, so many things to be said swirling around in my head. "It always surprised me that you could so easily forget them." I point back to the bar where our old friends still laugh inside. "And don't talk to me about things I already know. Back in the day, it was I who was going to make it out of here for the both of us."

Before my career had ended in eighty-five percent mobility in my knee, I was headed for the big leagues. Even had a contract on my desk, just looking to be signed. Our plan had been to travel the world, her by my side, me playing the sport I loved. It had all come crashing down, though.

Savannah is quiet and then begins fumbling in her purse. "You know what? If you're not going to talk about the house, if we can even call it that, then I'm going to go. I'll get a lawyer, we'll do this the hard way."

She sways a bit on the way to the car, and I swoop in quickly, taking the keys out of her hand. "You're not driving."

"Hey!" She swats at me, but I'm too tall compared to her sprite-like figure. "Give those back!"

"I'm not having you kill someone over a shack in the woods that saw our relationship's death." My eyebrows slope down at her. "Get in the truck."

Savannah sucks in her breath. I haven't told her to get in my truck in a long time. This used to be second nature for us.

"And do what? Listen to your bitching for the next ten minutes? No thank *you*." She exaggerates the last word.

"If you get in the truck, I'll discuss the house." Anything to keep her from killing herself, or someone else, on the road.

I watch as her petite, curvy frame saunters over, obliging happily once I mention her precious house. My God, she's always been the most beautiful thing my eyes have ever held. She's dressed like some slinky supermodel tonight, in expensive fabrics that cling to her skin. Her hair is fuller, and I want to wrap it around my fist. My cock hardens at just the slightest shimmy of her hips, and I'm reminded of just how long it's been without her. Without anyone.

Savannah walks around the bed of my truck and lets herself into the passenger seat, like she's done a thousand times before. I have to take a steadying breath before I step up onto the foot rail, because I know getting in there with her is going to wreck me even further.

And I'm one hundred percent correct. Her musky vanilla scent fills the cab like it's her own, and wraps around my brain. How many times did I lay her down in here, across the bench seat while our heads bumped the steering wheel? How many times did she moan my name on this scratchy leather?

My hands are shaking by the time I reach for my keys and start the engine.

The drive starts out relatively silent until a tipsy Savannah can't keep her thoughts in her head any longer. She was always so chatty with a few drinks in her.

"Gosh, I can't believe Cecily is married."

Keeping my eyes on the road, I nod. "Thomas is a good guy. She's very happy here."

Every one of my comments or statements is backhanded, and I know it doesn't slip past her notice. *Good.*

"And Jenks as the sheriff! I feel like I'm in the twilight zone." She chuckles.

"Don't we all? I'd have laughed my hide off if you told me a month ago that I'd be in my truck with Savannah Reese."

"It has been a long time, hasn't it?" I feel that pretty hazel stare burning a hole into the side of my face as I refuse to look at her.

"Why did you never pay for it? Sell it?" she asks in a hushed voice, as if she knows this is the most complicated of subjects.

And it is. Even more than our breakup, or my hatred for her leaving ... my reasons are my secrets alone.

Thankfully, we pull up to the house in that exact moment, and I'm saved by my opening door from answering.

The shack, *our* shack, looks the same as it always does. Decrepit. Ramshackle. Kind of like the relationship between us.

"Gosh, this place is a dump, isn't it? How did we ever think we could fix it up? We were so broke back then." She marvels at it under the moonlight.

And then an idea strikes me.

"I'll tell you what. You fix this house up, actually put in the work on something that means a damn to this town, and I'll buy it from you. You can walk, go back to your Yankee life and hoity-toity boyfriend."

Savannah's eyes swing to me, shock and surprise all over her face. Not only did I issue a gauntlet, but I mentioned the boyfriend. I know nothing about him, but I hate him anyway on principle.

"You'll buy it from me? That's rich. With what money? You know, since we owe about ten years of back taxes. I'll end up fixing it up and you'll still refuse to sell. How do I know this isn't a trick?"

She has no idea what I do now, how far I've come. And I won't tell her either. In her world, the one she's a part of now, money and power are the attractive things. Once upon a time, Savannah loved me for the man I was and the four nickels I had to rub together.

So instead of answering, I stick my hand out, wiggling the fingers.

In the moonlight, those hazel orbs recognize what I'm doing. Tentatively, like I might burn her when we touch, she puts the back of her hand to mine. We wiggle our fingers together, sliding the skin together until we're disconnected, and then swoop our pinkies in a dance only we know.

This is the handshake I made up with her in middle school when I was just trying to touch her in any way I could as a horny thirteen-year-old boy. We finish off with a high five, and Savannah is trying to bite back the smile forming on her lips.

"That seal it?" I ask, staring openly at her beauty.

She blinks like a deer in headlights. "Yeah."

I can't leave it without putting my real two cents in.

"There are a lot of people here that still love you. You left them behind, too. This is the last thing tying you to Hale, and you have no qualms about dumping it off your plate. You're not the girl I fell in love with."

Waiting a beat, baiting her, I stare intensely at Savannah. I just dropped the L word, and she's sitting there chewing it over.

But she's taking too long, this new version of her doesn't speak freely or come out with her honest thoughts. I don't like that, not one bit.

So I leave, waiting for her in the truck until she quietly climbs in a few minutes later.

The drive back to her sister's house is silent.

9

SAVANNAH

"Yes, Donna, I promise. I'll have the scripts to you in a month, I just won't be in New York to go over the lines with you each week."

The showrunner on the other end says something about communication, about collaboration.

"Come on, have you ever known me to miss a deadline? Have I ever not delivered the wow factor to you?" I try to put so much confidence in my voice that she can't say no.

Donna sighs loudly, but then relents, telling me I have three days to show her the first scenes. After promising I'll email them, I hang up with her and lean my head back against Adeline's couch.

Jesus, I can't believe I agreed to being stuck down here for a month. My clothes are already sticking to me, and it's only March. Plus, now I'll have to find time to work in this prison, with three kids around and no Starbucks in sight.

I've been working as the head writer on the biggest television drama for almost three years now. After working my way up in the industry, proving myself on guest writing roles or doing scenes for the measliest of commercials, I'd finally scored my big gig after Donna, the creator of *Love General*, watched one of my episodes on an army romantic comedy type show on network cable.

She'd loved the storyline, sought me out, and asked me to come write one episode of her wildly popular medical drama in a prime time slot on Thursday nights. I'd impressed her with that first script, and then just kept on doing so episode after episode. Now, we had a wonderful working relationship, but that would be hard to maintain now that I was stuck in the boondocks for a month, fixing up a house my ex-boyfriend should have sold a decade ago.

Being a writer did give me the freedom of working off location, though, so thankfully, I could still do what I loved while I tried to rectify this situation. And I did love it.

I've been writing since I was a little girl sitting in my bedroom in this town. Stories, so many stories, I always had one in my head. I'd narrate my life as I was doing it, creating scenarios for myself even if it was just getting off the bus after school. After my whole life fell apart and I made a break for it, I headed for New York, thinking I could live my dream. Once, when I was fourteen, I'd heard that writing TV shows was a job, and I'd been set on it since.

Little did I know, I'd nearly starve and nearly become homeless those first few years. I was a professional waitress, scribbling on notepads during my breaks and typing into the midnight hours to make my dream come true. I lived in a basement apartment with two roommates and slept on a futon in the living room. My only meals were peanut butter and bread, or what I could scrounge for free at my restaurant jobs.

Eventually, I made it, but not without years of strife. No one back here knew how hard it had been for me, but I did it all on my own, a fact I am proud of.

Now, I am the top writer on everyone's favorite doctor

romance drama, and I love absolutely everything about it. It pains me that I'll be away from my cast and crew, that I won't feel the energy on set to get inspired. But this is more important right now.

I can't believe Jason actually agreed, via handshake, to buy me out if I help fix the house up. I still feel like it's a trick, but handshake trumps all, so if he doesn't hold to his word, there will be hell to pay. Not that I know anything about fixing up a house, but I'll do just about anything to clear my credit and get back to Perry and our impending apartment sale right about now.

Just as I'm about to get up, to see who I could call to get my own place in this town, the front door swing opens.

And in walks my entire family.

Adeline, Brad, and the kids are followed by a tornado of four other screaming children, Noah and his girlfriend, Hope, and bringing up the rear is Lorelei. I know enough about my siblings to know that Noah and Hope will never get married, because they don't care about it even if they have kids together. And Lorelei's husband, Jameson, is at an army base somewhere in California for the next few months.

There is so much noise and chaos, I don't know where to look first. The kids swarm the house, pulling snacks off the shelves and running for toys, the backyard, and everything in between. Noah and Adeline are loudly discussing the merits of buying a new or used car, Lorelei is trying to quiet a very small baby in her arms, and Hope is carrying three pizzas before setting them down on the counter.

"Oh, Sav" Hope exclaims, jumping as if she's seen a ghost.

I hesitate to get up, because now they're all staring at me. "Uh, hi."

"Adeline told us you were here, but I thought she was

joking." Lorelei looks me up and down, the baby now falling asleep on her shoulder.

Lorelei and I are closest in age of all the siblings, but she's always been the cold one of us. A perpetually forgotten middle child, or so she dramatized herself as, Lori was always distant and unloving. It surprises me that she's had three children, and to see her with a baby is an odd sight.

"Nope, here I am. I didn't realize you were all coming by."

When I say this, Adeline turns away, and I know she set this up without telling me. I didn't want some kind of family reunion; it was awkward enough being here in her house.

"Well, we haven't seen you in forever. How are you, sis?" Noah comes over, grabbing me in a bear hug.

He looks so much like our dad that I feel an overwhelming sense of emotion and nostalgia. Growing up, he essentially *was* my dad. Our father passed when I was twelve, and it rocked our family. Our mother was left with four children on her own, and we all grieved differently for a parent we'd never see again.

Maybe that's when the cracks started. Clearly, they've all mended theirs, becoming this solid extended family. I envy it, how close they are with each other.

"I'm fine. I'll just uh, be in the guest room." I point to the hallway.

"No, no, I got more than enough pizza," Hope pipes up, always the peacemaker. "Come on, let's sit and eat."

Well, this couldn't be any more awkward. I feel like they're strangers, when we're all related by blood. I want to resist, but Adeline gives me this pleading look, so I walk over to the counter and wait to be given a plate so that I can serve myself pizza.

When we're all seated at the table, with the kids sitting on the living room floor all loudly talking over one another, Hope clears her throat.

"It's really nice to see you, Savvy. I just have to say, I watch every episode of *Love General*, and I think you're just so talented." She dazzles me with a smile.

Noah's longtime girlfriend has basically been another sister to me growing up and has always been bright and warm.

"Thanks, Hope. I love my job," I say simply, not sure how to do this.

"Addy didn't tell us why you're back in town. So why is that?" Lori looks to me as she bites off a piece of pepperoni, the baby snoozing in her lap.

No subtlety to be found there. "I'm trying to buy an apartment with my boyfriend in the city, and apparently still own that little house out on the lake. So I have to sell it before my credit score can clear for the sale."

Adeline snorts. "We all told you back then that investing in that craphole was a bad idea."

Hope giggles and covers Noah's hand where it lies on the table. "But it was so romantic."

"A boyfriend, huh? Why didn't he come with you?" Lori asks.

I stare at my pizza, not even hungry. It's hilarious how fast you can feel like the baby sister, even as an almost thirty-year-old, with all of your older siblings shooting questions at you.

"Perry is very busy, he works on Wall Street and just ... his job is very demanding."

And I didn't know how to, or didn't want to, introduce him to the world I grew up in. I see that unsaid answer all over their faces.

"Have you been out to see Mom?" Noah asks.

My sisters must have put him up to this, because they'd never be brave enough to ask. The table grows silent, the sorest of subjects causing my heart to fracture.

"No." I glower at him.

I have no intention of going out there to see her. There was a reason I hadn't been back to Hale in ten years.

Noah just took our family reunion from awkward to terrible. Why did they all have to push this issue? Before I left, they were down my throats about how I was feeling, what I needed to be myself again.

No one ever listened to me, just like no one was listening to me now.

Indeed, a month was going to be a very long time to be back in my hometown. I was definitely going to have to get my own place to escape to.

10

SAVANNAH

Three days later, I unpack the third and last suitcase I had shipped here from New York.

The apartment I'm renting, above The Whistlestop, isn't anything to write home about. It's decor is from the 1980s, there are no walls separating the kitchen from the bedroom or bedroom from the living room, and it's sad that I'm thankful I have a door on the bathroom.

But Rudy's daughter kept it clean, put fresh sheets on the bed, and the whole place smells of delicious coffee, so I guess it's not a horrible place to rest my head. And I've slept in worse places, felt more unsafe than I do. Not that I'd ever feel unsafe in Hale, it's the sleepiest little town on the planet.

From the moment I made that deal with Jason, I knew I'd need my own place for the next month. I couldn't stand one more day of Adeline's curious stares, or the questions she wasn't asking. I needed silence, peace, for my own sanity.

And no more questions about my mother.

I've been sitting down for about an hour, trying to get some work done, when the scent of the espresso tempts me beyond what I'm capable of fighting. Packing up my laptop, I head downstairs, in search of one of those great cappuccinos. Hopefully, Jason isn't the one making them, and I'm relieved when it's just Rudy down in the shop during this late afternoon hour.

After we chat for a minute and he takes my order, I choose a table in the corner by the window, set my blueberry muffin and laptop up, and proceed to write.

I'm in the middle of one of the males on the show professing his love for his superior female doctor in the middle of a chaotic surgery when I hear my name across the shop.

Before I know what's happening, Cecily is bouncing toward me.

"Oh my gosh, so good to see you again!" She bends down, hugging my neck.

And then just sits across from me at my table. Like I've invited her. Like I'm not trying to get some work done.

"Oh, um, hey Cecily. I was actually—"

Rudy cuts me off from trying to get her up from that seat, by setting down my cappuccino and the coffee Cecily must have ordered. "So good to see you two back together, sitting in my shop."

His crinkly smile warms my heart, and I don't have the chops to tell Cecily to hightail it out of here anymore. Closing my laptop, I resign myself to a late night accomplishing what I need to get to Donna.

"You doing okay? I know it must be strange to be back here."

Her question surprises me, and the sincerity of her tone, like she knows me, catches me off guard. I forget that she does know me, probably better than most people who have come and gone through my life.

She's also the first person to ask me how I'm actually doing. "Um, I'm all right. It's weird being back in town. Seeing Jason. Seeing my family. I never meant to stay away for so long, but I guess being in New York just made me feel ... healed?"

Cecily nods sadly. "I won't say I haven't missed you. But I knew you had to go. What happened was inconceivable. No one blames you for that, Savvy."

I snort. "You wouldn't think that by their comments and attitudes."

She shrugs. "Your family is hurt that you stayed away. You missed their lives, and I won't sugarcoat that. You missed mine. I want you to be happy, believe me, I do. But there are a lot of people here that love you."

She's the second person this week to say those words to me. They hit deep, in a place I've long forgotten about. Part of me feels so cold, never returning or speaking to people who had been my entire world. But they just didn't understand what was going on in my head. And by the time I truly reconciled it all, I was a different person.

I'd grown up this sweet, wild girl with as much chaos in my soul as a summer thunderstorm. I trusted too easily, listened to what I was supposed to, loved fiercely, and against all odds. I was naive and young.

New York has made me jaded. Distant. I protect my heart now, and yet coming back here, I can see that all of these people remain the same way I knew them. They're open and compassionate, they talk about everything and don't hesitate to hug or lend a hand. I feel like an alien in this world now.

"Anyways," Cecily clears her throat, "tell me about your fella!"

She's changing the subject mercifully to help me out, and I jump at the chance. Back in the day, girl talk was our number one favorite activity.

"Perry is a trader on Wall Street, so he's really successful at his job. He's smart, loves to take me to exotic restaurants, and just knows so much about the world. We love to go to Broadway plays together, and he has season tickets to Yankee Stadium."

Cecily cocks her head, a weird expression filling her delicate features, and I realize that none of the words out of my mouth were about Perry as a man or our relationship.

"Also, he's really good to me. He makes me a better person." The addition seems desperate and hasty.

"So, y'all ain't getting married, but you're moving in together? Seems history does repeat itself." She smirks, not in a sardonic way but in a joking manner.

Because back when Jason and I told everyone we were shacking up, literally, there were a lot of people up in arms about us not being married. The people in my hometown will curse on holidays, get drunker than Charlie Sheen at their kid's graduation parties, but God forbid someone moves in together before walking down the aisle at the local church.

"Yep." I nod, smiling.

I don't feel like going into the specifics, mostly because ... well, Perry and I haven't really talked about it. I could barely get him to relinquish control on his bachelor ways and move in with me, I wasn't pushing marriage. Sure, I've thought about it. My parents had one of the best marriages I've ever seen, and I always thought I'd have the same.

Never in my life did I think I'd be thirty, unmarried, and childless. Growing up where I did, I just didn't think that was going to be my future. Now that I'm here, I'm not terribly upset about it, but I'd like our relationship to be progressing faster than it has. I don't even know if Perry wants children, I've always been too scared to broach the subject.

Some would say it's terrible to move in with a man, to buy a home with him, if you don't know explicitly what he wants for the future. I'm going to own property with another human, and what if he tells me a year from now that he has no desire to be a father. I'd be shattered.

But like everything else in my life, I close up my feelings and lock them away tight. It's just easier that way.

"Tell me, do Danny and Veronica end up back together? I just have to know!" Cecily asks about the main couple on my show, *Love General.*

That makes me chuckle. "Well, now, I can't tell you that! You'll just have to keep watching."

You wouldn't believe how many people who know what I do ask me on a daily basis about the outcome of their favorite show.

"It's really good to have you back here, Sav."

Cecily reaches across the table and squeezes my hand. And for the first time since I've been back, a little glimmer of home passes through my bones.

"It's really good to see you, Ceci," I tell her, because it's true.

I haven't allowed myself to think about what my alternate life would have looked like, had I stayed in Hale. But for just one second, I see it as it could have been.

And I mourn for the happiness I could have had here.

11

JASON

Beau lugs one more barrel onto the shelves with me, both of us sputtering with exertion.

Sweat drips down our faces, and I hand him a water bottle from the cooler without any words. We chug, hauling in breaths until we can see straight again.

"Fuck, don't ask me to do this again," he curses at me.

"Hey, I work for free on your line. Least you can do for me is lug barrels in during the off season," I admonish him.

He shrugs. "I don't need your labor. You're free."

Rolling my eyes, I snort. "Yeah right, I'm better than any of your guys and you know it."

I run a hand down the smooth wood of the cabernet we just loaded onto a shelf. The stock we have aging for summer is going to be incredible, and a tingle goes down my spine.

It's my fourth year owning Darling June Vineyards, and this is going to be our best year yet, I can feel it. The harvest was especially plentiful; we have some new machines and techniques with this year's batch of wines, and our publicity is up since we'd been covered on a hometown vineyard show on a big network television channel.

At the tail end of our season, before we closed for summer, we had such an influx of tourist customers coming from places as far away as California that they tripled our sales for the year.

The former Hale Vineyards was owned by a family for over fifty years, before the parents passed in old age and the children decided to sell. I scraped up the money for the loan, because I knew I could make this place something special. It was my shot to make something of myself, to give back to the town I love. And I'd done it ... or I was on the way to doing it. My winery is now a go-to spot for locals, tourists, and families alike. We threw two summer festivals, held private parties and tastings, and even put on two weddings last year.

In the winter months, it's basically just maintenance for me. Looking over the vines, managerial tasks, and catering to a handful of local festivals and two or three private events. I spend a lot of time thinking up new ideas for the winery, marketing it, and just poring over the books. It's why I have so much time to volunteer around here, because let's face it, I wasn't spending my time doing anything but working one place or another.

Darling June Vineyards is my pride and joy, and I won't lie, it has made me more comfortable than I ever thought I'd be in my life financially.

"I'm just glad that's done. Now, do I get a free glass or what?" My best friend walks over to the bottles in the cellar.

We're standing in the enormous wine cellar beneath the building, that houses all of our stock and aging barrels. "Hey, hands off that stuff. I'll get you one from the stock upstairs, but first, I have to go look at this break in one of the fences out in the vines."

He grumbles behind me but follows, and soon we're standing on top of the hill, in rows of vines, overlooking the lake. It's a view that will steal your breath, and one of my favorite places in the entire world. Part of that has to do with the fact that it's mine.

Well, almost mine. By the end of next season, it'll be mine. Though, it might take another year or two now that I have to buy off the house from Savannah and pay all the property taxes I've been avoiding, like a total moron.

We're inspecting the break, just a consequence of winter, when Beau nods his head toward the end of the row, where Noah Reese stands. Well, should have been expecting this one.

"Noah, how you doing?" I shake his hand as I come to stand next to him.

"Good, Jay. This place is looking good. Getting ready for season?" he asks.

I nod. "Can't wait to get this place up and running again. It's my favorite time of year."

"Hope and I can't wait to resume our weekly date night here. She loves that chocolate and cheese pairing you guys do." He chuckles.

"It's a favorite," I agree. "What can I do for you?"

Noah sighs, but he's always been an upfront guy. Even before Savannah left, we'd formed a friendship. It was weird at first, seeing her family around town after we broke up. But eventually, we all just became citizens of the same town, and Noah and I have grabbed a beer now and then at Buddy's.

"I'm sure you've seen Savannah. I know why she's back here, and what you guys are fighting over."

If he's going to try to fight her battle for her, he's come to lose. But what he says next surprises me.

"And I just want you to ... you've got to get her back, Jay. I haven't even seen you two together yet, and I know there is still so much love between you. Out of us all, you were the two that were supposed to make it. It kills me that she ran away, that she barely talks to her family or knows her nieces and nephews. She loves you, always has. You need to make a big play here, pull out all the stops. I'll help you in any way I can, but she has to stay this time."

I feel dazed after he finishes. "Shit, I did not think *that* is what you were going to say. And I have to tell you, man, I'm not sure that any of that is true or is going to happen. She has a life, a boyfriend back in New York. She barely wants anything to do with me and has told me as much. Believe me, if I thought there was a chance in hell, I'd ... I'd try."

It's the first time I've ever told anyone in town of how badly I want Savannah back. Sure, they probably all know it, but I haven't declared my feelings.

"How does it feel when you're with her? Just out of curiosity," Noah presses me.

I shake my head, looking off into the distance. "Like the first time I ever saw her. Magical and fated. It's how I always feel when I'm around her."

He pats me on the shoulder. "You can't let her go, Jay. We're all counting on you. Bring our girl home."

Then Noah leaves just as abruptly as he swept in.

Walking back to where I was working, I'm even more messed up about the whole situation than I was before.

"What did he want?" Beau asks, though he was probably eavesdropping on our entire conversation.

"For me to win his sister back." I grunt, using pliers to remove the broken part of wire from the grapes it's already destroyed.

My best friend goes still. "Do you want to win her back?"

Savannah has been a sore subject between us for years. Beau thinks she's a selfish asshole, and he even knows the full story. Her leaving town was unforgivable to him, but I see the other side. I was at fault, too.

"I've loved the woman my entire life. You know that. If I thought there was a chance ... yes. I'd try."

"She broke your heart."

"Yeah, and I wasn't the most innocent in the situation either. I was a selfish, heartless prick when she needed me the most. Back then, I was so wrapped up in my injury and not being able to play anymore that I wasn't there for her."

"You were kids," Beau insists.

"We were soul mates. Probably still are," I challenge.

He sighs, knowing he won't win this one. "I just don't want you to be more fucked-up than you already are over her. If you can't convince her to stay, if she doesn't pick you? I don't want to see that for you, my friend."

I know he means well, but so does every friend, relative, or person who tries to give you advice on love.

The thing is, your heart is always going to do whatever the hell it wants. Even if it means it's going to get broken.

12

SAVANNAH

Pulling up to the house, our house, in the daylight is a different kind of torture.

Since Cecily's kindness, all the things I used to love about Hale have come creeping back into my mind. The holidays spent here, the summer fair we'd all flock to, the endless days of a warm winter spent daring each other to jump in the lake. I remember cuddling on the couch with my family for our mandatory Friday movie nights, and all the things that happened between Jason and me.

There was a time when I never would have left Hale for anything, and when I put my car in park at the property we own together, ghosts of the past whisper in my ear.

"I see you still have the same penchant for running about twenty minutes late."

His voice hits me as soon as I cross the threshold, though I didn't see Jason's truck when I pulled up. He always did have this mysterious way of sneaking up on me.

"A woman has to keep her charms, isn't that right?" I say coyly, running my pointer finger over the dusty surfaces.

"I wouldn't say what you are is necessarily charming." He scoffs sarcastically.

Finally, I turn to face him, and I immediately wish I hadn't. Um, what he's wearing should be illegal. It's a miracle my jaw doesn't unhinge, it's hanging open so wide.

Leaning against the doorframe like some kind of sexy lumberjack model is Jason, in an olive-green thermal shirt that molds to his biceps and pecs in all the right places. His jeans are scuffed and ripped, though not in the style that looks like they've come from a store. No, these are the type earned by hammering roofs together and kneeling in the mud to change a tire. Paired with chunky Timberland boots, Jason looks like some kind of cover model for a country music album. And then there is the rumpled, just-slept-in head of midnight-black locks, and the eyes that hooked me a long time ago.

Those baby blues, as innocent as they are devilish, could put the Texas stars to shame.

He does the same slow perusal of my body. I opted for black leggings and a long white tunic long sleeve, with my hair piled into a ponytail. I may be more into fashion and labels than I was when I left here, but I know when I'm coming to do manual labor. I'll never be one of those girls who shows up to help someone fix something in heels and a blouse.

"So, where are we starting?" I ignore him, looking around.

There are two major holes in the drywall near two windows, I noticed a panel of roofing missing, and the floors need to be refinished, though not replaced. I'm sure the place could use new windows and some appliance upgrades if we really want to list it for top dollar, but the bones of it are surprisingly good.

Jason must have surmised all of this, because he points to the drywall. "We need to completely remove those two panels, put in new drywall, and then paint the whole room a fresh coat of—"

"A nice soft gray. I've already picked the paint, it's in my car. I have some for the bedroom too, and the bathroom as well," I tell him.

His eyebrows shoot up, like he's surprised I'm putting any kind of thought into this.

"Oh, don't act like you're shocked. I've always been good following through on projects. If this means I'm one step closer to going home, then I'm going all in."

Walking to the damaged wall, I run my hand over the holes, and then select a sledgehammer from Jason's toolbox on the floor.

"Do you even know how to use that thing?" Jason asks me.

While I fully anticipate hiring a decorator for the new apartment, because I can afford it, I did do all the hanging and handiwork in my first place, and my current upgrade of an apartment. I didn't have a dad or a boyfriend, sheesh I barely had friends who would help me stuff my things into a cab and carry them up the three flights of stairs. If a lightbulb needed changing, a sink needed fixing, a hole needed patching, I'm the one who did it.

"It looks pretty self-explanatory, plus I have a lot of anger I need to take out. Should be fun." I wink at him before turning and ramming the tool into the wall.

Chunks of sawdust, bits of particle and all sorts of other things fly into the air, and subsequently, into my eyes. Coughing as if I'll never reach my next breath, I blink against the burning in my eyes. My entire body feels like it's been flung into a desert; I can't see, the entire world is dry and I'm about to pass out.

"Come here." Strong hands grab me by the shoulders, and the next moment I feel water drench my face.

The relief is staggering, so much so that I cling to the only thing keeping me upright—Jason. I feel wind on my face, and as I rapidly blink my eyes against the debris inside them, his breath blowing the matter out is soothing and calming.

After another minute, I've regained the use of my faculties, but lean against him still, allowing him to blow gently into my eyes. His mouth is in a circle, his whole face concentrated on helping me, on making sure I'm okay. Somewhere inside my chest, my heart bows and bends, stretching the muscle I've not used for a long time.

See, my love with Perry is an intellectual one, it's all from the brain. I know he's a good man; I understand that I'm better when I'm with him; the explanation of why we should be together is one of fact and reasonable conclusion.

With Jason? It's all instinct. All heart. No logic and no rational thought; our souls love each other on a level that is kismet. There will never be a time that my heart won't belong to him, and it knows it.

That's why I've been trying to fight it for so long.

"Are you okay?" he asks, genuine concern marking his features.

I stare up at him in a daze, blinking slowly, wondering how our mouths got to be just inches from each other.

"I am now." My voice is thin, since his arms are still wrapped around me.

Jason releases me abruptly. "Well, guess that answers my question about how much you know when it comes to demolition and construction. Next time you decide to pick up a tool, moron, put on some safety goggles. I don't need to come to your rescue again."

His voice is so harsh and unrelenting, it pierces the heart that just yearned for him. I'm embarrassed, my cheeks flaming red, because I just made myself look so naive and inexperienced. Meanwhile, I was the one who got out and lived on a grander scale than him. And in two seconds, I'd accomplished making myself look like a total idiot.

"You're an ass," I mumble, grabbing the goggles he just tossed at me and putting them on.

For the next two hours, we work in silence. I bust up the wall, my arms wobbling by the end of the destruction of one panel. But hell, does it feel good. Smashing that wood over and over again, picturing all the fucked-up things that happened in this town ... it's kind of therapeutic.

Jason clears the other panel in half the time I did, and then disappears, until I hear him on the roof. When I'm done, I walk to my car, pulling the water bottle and granola bar from my passenger seat as I watch Jason scale down the roof like a ninja.

"Roof is done. We'll need to get those new panels of drywall up tonight, and then tomorrow come back to paint. I can refinish the floors, which will take some time, and then ordering new windows will take about a week. Then it's just the ... inside touches."

Inside touches is code for girly shit, which he apparently has deemed my area of expertise.

"Well, where is the drywall?" I ask.

Jason snorts. "I have to go pick some up. Here's the deal. You grab us lunch, and I'll head to the Home Depot in Wachot."

He climbs into his truck and starts it, clearly intent on heading to the home supply store two towns over.

"What do you want to eat?" I scramble, panicking.

Not that I want to buy him lunch, but I want to keep him in a good mood. The more we tackle at the house, the quicker I get to sell my half to him and get the hell back to New York.

He leans out the window, one elbow on the door, a sly smile on those full lips.

"If you don't remember my sandwich order, then you never really knew me at all."

13

JASON

By the time I get back with the two pieces of drywall and the floor refinishing machine I rented from Home Depot, Savannah is setting up a picnic of sorts.

She has two sandwiches from Rounding Home, unwrapped and sitting on their mounds of paper. Tiny containers of oil and vinegar, mayonnaise, hot peppers, and relish sit in the middle. There is a fountain drink of sweet tea in her place, while I have a Mountain Dew in mine.

Back in the day, we used to do this all the time. Sometimes, even in this very spot. As eighteen-year-olds who decided to move in together, we didn't have much. A mattress on the floor, an old TV someone was throwing out that we picked up off the side of the road, a busted DVD player, and a lumpy blue leather couch. We had no kitchen table, no chairs, and little else.

Of course, we had a grand plan to buy all these things, but then Savannah had bolted, and I boarded this place up to rot.

"Glad to see you can at least remember one thing about me." I tilt my head to the sandwich.

"A turkey, roast beef, and provolone with extra jalapeños,

honey mustard, lettuce, and tomato on wheat bread," she recites.

"And a tuna and white American for you, with extra oregano," I say back.

We stare at each for a moment, and then I move to sit on the floor. Savannah looks uncomfortable, like how she's set this up is a mistake. Honestly, I'm expecting her to grab hers and make some excuse about eating in her car while taking a phone call, but then she sits down.

I bite into my sandwich, realizing I'm hungrier than I thought I was. She does the same, looking anywhere but at me.

"So, you really did it, huh?" I start in, attempting to make conversation.

We've done nothing but pick each other apart or stare in miserable silence since she came back to Hale, and if I am going to try to make anything happen—even a friendship—I am going to have to wave a white flag ... somewhat.

"What?" Those big hazel orbs blink up at me.

"Your writing, you really turned it into something. Not that I watch the show; I still don't have cable. But people around here rave about it." I try to pay her a compliment.

Savannah chuckles. "Of course, you don't have cable."

I shrug. "I catch games at Buddy's, and everything else, well, I don't really need to see."

"What the heck do you do with all of your other time, then?" She cocks her head to the side, curious.

"Work," I say simply.

Savannah looks skeptical. "At The Whistlestop? What, with Beau? I'm sorry, I just ... I never pegged you as the guy who would settle into Hale's fix-it man role."

What she doesn't say is that when she knew me, I had the biggest dreams of all. Starting pitcher for the Texas major league team. Endorsement deals. Hall of fame career. Those had been my goals, and I'd never been the guy to settle. I'd been a cocky little shit, unaware of how much the baseball system can chew you up and spit you out. Until it happened to me.

And now, she thinks I'm some bum who borrows jobs from people who know I need money. It couldn't be further from the truth, but I'm not about to brag on my accomplishments when she thinks so low of me.

"Something like that. So, you're all Hollywood now?" I turn the subject back to her.

Those hazel eyes give me one last searching look and then turn to amusement. "Not quite. Yes, I have an agent, and I make a salary I never dreamed I would, but I'm not Hollywood. No one knows who the writers are, they just create the show and it's magic but get little of the credit. I'm more than fine with it that way, I just want to dream up stories."

"You always did," I say softly, remembering how she'd always be scribbling on napkins at the diner or errant pieces of notebook paper in class.

"I'm living my dream." She sighs dreamily, but I see the reservation there, too.

"And the boyfriend? You're ... happy?" It's like taking a knife to the gut to say those words.

She avoids eye contact. "Very. He's good for me."

Good *for* me, not *to* me. I don't miss the word choice.

"Well then, I'm happy for you. It's probably a good thing you didn't stay here, with me. We were a bunch of hooligan teens, thinking we could live here and fix it up."

I chew a bite, trying to let the lightness of my voice invade my black soul, but it's not working. Apparently, you can't always fake it till you make it.

Savannah looks around the tiny home. "Yeah, we sure were full of ourselves. But there was something so innocent and exciting about it. We really thought we were going to make it."

"I would have bet money on it, darling."

Her intake of breath is so sharp, I'm expecting to see frostbite on her lips.

I haven't used the endearment since she's been back, and it just slipped out. I wouldn't have used it on purpose, but being here, talking about what we were supposed to be, has me all kinds of messed up.

She doesn't say anything, and so I press my luck, furthering the issue. "Listen, Savvy, I never apologized for that week. I was so blind with what happened with the injury that I couldn't see past myself. I shouldn't have said those things, I should have been at the funeral. Your mom meant—"

"*No.*" The word is so hard it feels like a smack. "I'm not talking about this."

And just like that, she gets up, retreating from the house. I hear the BMW's engine start, and then the gravel spray as she peels out.

I should have known. It was the reason she left Hale, so I should have known that she hasn't dealt with it in the ten years we've been apart. Her mother was her world, June Reese was everyone's world.

After cleaning up the food, I put up both pieces of drywall and refinish the bedroom floors, working late into the night to keep my mind off of everything I shouldn't have said.

14

SAVANNAH

I'm about to throw a pint of chocolate chip cookie dough into my basket when I hear my name down the aisle.

"Sav!"

Turning to see who else is in the grocery store—I knew I should have come at seven a.m. when they opened or right before they closed to avoid seeing anyone I knew—I see my sister Lori, her three kids, and Hope.

Well, I can't necessarily bolt now; it would only make me appear worse than most of my siblings thought I already was. Especially Lori.

"Hey." I give them a little wave, and we meet in the middle of the aisle.

The kids, two boys and the baby strapped to Lori's chest, look at me like I'm any other stranger. Back in the day, I thought I'd have about five kids before I was thirty. I wanted to be a mother so badly. But after everything that happened, and living with Perry in New York, now I wasn't so sure.

But seeing them stare at me, feelings of guilt and sadness mix in my stomach to form a nauseating combination. I should know them. I should wake up with them on Christmas mornings and go to their school plays.

I could live in my blissfully ignorant bubble as long as I never thought about the people in this place. I could go through life ignoring my issues. But now that I'm here, it's all laid out in front of my face, an insult to everything I've built. Because in reality, I have nothing. I'm a workaholic dating a workaholic, grinding to make more money and more money each year. I have friends that I don't really like, and I'm constantly trying not to think about the past.

"How are you doing? Did you start work on the house today?" Hope asks, cheerful as ever.

"Yeah, I'm exhausted. Earned this whole pint of ice cream," I joke.

"That's Mommy's favorite flavor, too!" one of the little boys says.

It kills me that I don't remember his name.

I smile at him. "I know, we used to split whole cartons when we were kids. We would sneak them into the bedroom we shared."

Lorelei looks at me in shock, clearly thinking prior to this moment I have no good memories of her.

"That's right, we did." The smallest of smiles forms on her lips. "We're um ... we're getting the ingredients for chicken Parmesan for dinner. Would you ... like to join us for dinner?"

It's a big gesture she's making here, but I'm so physically and emotionally drained, I know I won't be good company.

"That's really nice of you, but I'm just so tired. We replaced two panels of drywall today, my arms feel like jelly. I'll probably shovel some of this ice cream in my face and then pass out. But ... maybe sometime this week?"

Something about being back in that house with Jason, with him mentioning my mama, reminded me of how fleeting our time together is. Not just because I will leave to go back to New York, but because last time I left ... I couldn't say goodbye to one of them.

Honestly, I almost start tearing up in the grocery store.

God dammit, I just wanted to get home and eat my freaking ice cream and try not to cry. It's been a shit day, my heart is in shambles, and the last thing I want to do is run into my family.

Families make you talk, especially mine. They want to hash shit out, talk about our feelings, and heal together. I used to want no part of that, and I was still hesitant.

When my mother died, I was angry at the entire world. I was furious at my siblings for getting more time with her than I ever would. I was pissed off that the universe took her from me, robbing me of a long life with, not to mention, my mother but my father, too.

The person I was most mad at, though, was myself. I'd nearly broken her heart when I told her I was moving out and into the tiny house with Jason. She thought we were rushing, that we were too young. I was also her last baby, and she wasn't ready to let me go. I didn't listen to any of it. I said things that came out of the mouth of someone young and inexperienced in the ways of life. At the time of her death, we'd barely been speaking.

I wanted to die when she died. My mama had been *the best* mother. Tough but fair, loving, and always willing to lend an ear. She made hundreds of Christmas cookies for neighbors during the holidays, rocked babies left up for adoption at the local hospital once a week, and always volunteered at our schools. June Reese was the epitome of southern class and comfort, and I wanted to be just like her.

When she passed suddenly, just six months after I graduated high school, I couldn't handle it. Couple that with Jason's breakdown, and I had no choice but to run.

I got out of Hale as fast as I could and never looked back. I never stopped grieving or blaming myself.

"That's fine." Lori's expression shutters, and I know I've lost any openness I'd earned from her.

I'd kick myself later, right now I am just so bone tired.

"Can you come over next week, though?" the other little boy asks me.

"You bet. I'll cook. You guys like tacos?" I ask them, not bothering to clear with Lori.

"Yeah!" they cry in unison.

"You got it, then," I tell them.

"Come on boys, we have to go to the deli." Lori ushers them away. "See you later, Sav."

At least she's addressing me by name now.

"Sav, I need to talk to you about Mama." Hope lingers behind, referring to my mother like she's her own.

Just like Jason, Hope had been basically been taken in by my mom. She was the one who made sure both of them had hot meals on school nights, that if they didn't have a place to sleep, the couch was made up for them. Mama was the one who drove Jason to his first agent's meetings, and she'd been the one to take Hope to the gynecologist when it was time for her first visit.

Hope was as much a sister as my two blood ones, but she had a unique perspective. Maybe it's why I listened to her, why I didn't sprint away right there, leaving my cart full of groceries in the middle of the Piggly Wiggly.

I'm shaking like a leaf as I nod, because everything in me is fighting against the urge to scream that *no, I don't want to hear this*.

"Every other Sunday, we go to visit her grave, obviously Daddy's, too. And then we have a big family dinner. We'd love for you to join this week. I know how hard this is for you, but we'd all like to talk about it. We miss her so much, too, Sav. But it helps to be together."

They probably all sent her, the angel among us, because she'd have the best shot.

I have to fight through the knot in my throat. "I'm glad you all get together to honor her. I really am, truly that's not sarcasm. I just ... I can't, Hope."

"You have to stop blaming yourself, Sav. It was a heart attack, nothing you did. She knew how much you loved her. We all know that."

"Did she?" I whisper, looking away.

After a moment, I clear my throat. "I have to go. You guys have a good night, okay."

I get out of the Piggly Wiggly as quickly as possible, and when I get home, the ice cream goes untouched.

Not even Ben & Jerry can help this emotional hangover.

15

JASON

It's another two days before Savannah contacts me—maybe she still has my number, that I hadn't changed since high school, or maybe someone gave it to her—to go back and work on the house.

For someone who says they want nothing more than to sell and get out of Hale, she sure is taking her time. Though, I know how difficult it was for her to hear her mama's name. To hear the nickname her father used to call her mother, the one we used to joke I'd call her when we got married.

Darling. Leonard Reese called his wife that for over twenty years, and when we would lie in our field, the one just past the hill up from this house, we'd dream about that being us one day. Married with a couple of kids, settled and calling each other old southern endearments like darlin'.

Since she dropped off the radar two days ago, I've been working day and night to get these floors done. In reality, I should be stalling the process, doing all I can to delay us and keep her here for longer. I still haven't figured out a plan to make her stay, or if I want to.

Of course, I want Savannah. I've never not wanted her. I've

been in love with the woman since I could have a crush on a girl. Still though, I'm not over her leaving me behind. What I did was wrong, but what she did was worse.

The day I tore both my MCL and ACL in my right knee was about three weeks before June Reese shockingly died. I was at a practice, a clinic of sorts for players entering the draft or being recruited into the farm system for a major league team. I was pushing so hard, whipping pitches and running through sprint and hitting drills so quick that it practically felt like my body was on fire.

Pain, hot and venomous, licked up my thigh, down to my toes, and I knew. I was done. They didn't even have to bring the doctor in, his expression trying to remain cold and unaffected as he told me that I would never play baseball professionally. Later, I'd learn that my right leg would only have eighty-five percent mobility in it, which is why, if you knew what happened, you could detect the slight limp that now accompanies me everywhere.

After that, I couldn't see past my own fury. I was fucking pissed at the world, at anyone who looked at me or spoke to me. I treated Savvy like shit, was a terrible patient and boyfriend, completely failed her as her human.

And then, in the middle of my depression and breakdown, June died. It was a complete and utter shock and hit the entire community so hard. No one more than Savannah, though. She was the baby, and she and her mom had disagreed about us moving in together into the tiny house by the lake.

I couldn't be there for her, not properly. I was still so damaged from my injury, still on bedrest and awaiting surgery to repair all the broken parts of my leg. Savannah retreated into herself, lashing out at random times, and then I'd do the same. We were the worst versions of ourselves, and it was a dark time.

So you see, I was the asshole, the piece of crap boyfriend

who wasn't there on the hardest day of her life. But Savannah didn't fight for us at all. She just threw in the towel. She abandoned me too, at one of the hardest times in my life, and never looked back. I tried for weeks to call her, I even ... I went to New York a couple months after.

But I knew it was over for her.

Nursing that heartbreak took a good year-long bender, after which Beau sat me down and told me it was time to put the past in the past. He sobered me up, Rudy took me in, and slowly, I became a man worth something again.

I want to be enough for her. I want her to choose me. And I know she needs proof and coaxing before that happens, but there is this block in my head I can't get past. She carries a grudge toward me, we all know that. But what I didn't consider until she came back is that I have one for her still lingering on my shoulders.

When Savannah shows up, about thirty minutes after I arrive, I'm already putting the first coat of paint on the walls. There is a second roller in the tray, and wordlessly, she sheds her coat and then walks over to pick it up.

We're basically ignoring each other, going about our work like prison inmates forced to work on the same task. It's uncomfortable, and all I want to do is push her buttons. A yelling Savannah is better than a quiet Savannah any day.

"Are we going to talk about the other day? Or am I never allowed to mention your mother again?" I turn to her abruptly, my voice slicing through the peace of the forest and lake.

Shit, I mean, I could have led with something gentler than that. Plus, Savannah has a paintbrush in her hand, and this can only end badly.

"You had to bring her up? Really? Again? I told you no!" Savannah shouts, every muscle in her perfect body going rigid.

She's a hurricane of anger headed straight toward me. And I love it.

"Yeah, I did. Because I miss her too, and I need to apologize for not being there for you. I was a shitty, selfish loser, and I should have caught you when you fell. To this day, it's my biggest regret in life." I push right back, my chest puffing out and my chin jutting.

This is it, this is where we thrive. On the brink of chaos, with lust and love and passion swirling around us in a heated, electric storm.

"You have no right! You fucked it all up!" She throws down the brush, paint splattering onto her clothes.

"Yeah, and you left!" I yell back, getting fired up.

This was bound to happen, the snap, and I brought it on. Good. I want to see her pissed off. I want to let my rage out.

"Because the one person I counted on to hold me up when she died was nowhere in sight! I'm not doing this, I'm not getting into this." She crosses her arms and then pushes them out, as if this motion will make the conversation end.

"Then when will we do this? Jesus Christ, Savannah, you've avoided having this conversation for ten fucking years!" I shout.

There is so much pain between us, so much unforgiven shit and love that has no idea where to exist anymore.

"You know what, you're right." Her face is a mask of indignant rage. "You didn't love me enough to put me before yourself! Before your goddamn sport!"

She screams bloody murder, the crux of the issue coming out.

My voice goes deadly quiet. "There has never been a day that I've stopped loving you. Over the last ten years, I've convinced myself I will die a lonely man, simply because I will never feel about another person the way I do about you. Then you blow back into town, and I swear to God, Savannah, my heart started beating again. And so, if I never get another chance to do this, I'm taking it now."

Without waiting another second, I crush my lips to hers.

I half expect her to slap me across the face, or scream into my mouth. But I'm met with the same fever pitch of wanting that I pour into her mouth. We're two humans so miserably and ill-fatedly in love with each other that each second of this kiss hurts, but also makes us feel like the world is on fire because of the flames we're producing.

Savannah grabs the back of my neck, allowing me to haul her up and against me. My eyes are closed and I'm frantically plunging my tongue into her mouth as she returns the dance, but I walk us to the wall, needing something to steady us.

When her back collides with it, neither of us caring if it's a section with fresh paint or not, Savannah's hands leave my neck and search for the hem of my shirt.

Up and over my head it goes, everything moving so fast that it actually feels like we're moving in slow motion. Like if you can't see us with your naked eye, this can't actually be happening.

My hands mold to her breasts, rubbing over her nipples as they bud through the bra and thin cotton shirt she wears. I long to feel all of her, to take her under me and make love to her. Show her all the ways I've desperately missed her in the past ten years.

"Oh my God." Savannah breaks off, pushing against me.

I exhale, a whoosh of energy and adrenaline deflating my stomach. My arms bracket her head, searching that beautiful face for any sign of hope. I'm shirtless, she's mussed, and we're both breathing like we just ran a marathon.

"We can't ... fuck, I shouldn't be doing this. I have a boyfriend."

"I don't care." I'm not even sorry for saying it.

"Well, I do! This makes me a cheater. You just made me a cheater. As if you haven't hurt me enough." She wipes the back of her hand across her mouth, an expression of dismay and unbelievability in her hazel eyes.

"You don't love him. Don't you feel this?" I grab her hand and smash it to my chest.

I'm so wrapped up in the moment, dangling off the cliff, that I might as well go for it all. If I plummet to my death, so be it.

"That doesn't ... it isn't the only thing. Love isn't enough." She throws her hands up incredulously.

"Love is the only thing. If you haven't learned that after all these years, then ..." I trail off, not sure how I can get through to her.

She belongs here, in Hale. She belongs with me. But she'll never admit it.

"I have to go." Savannah ducks under my arm.

With one backward look, a split second where I think she might jump into my arms again, she does what she does best.

She walks out on me.

16

SAVANNAH

"What're you doing?"

A curious little voice comes from next to me, where Delilah, Adeline's oldest daughter, plops down on the couch. Delilah is eleven and acts like I do at my age. She's a fierce little thing, having the most contact with me since I came into town. The one thing my sister's oldest child keeps saying is that she can't wait to bust out of Hale.

"I'm trying to write a script for my show." I smile at her, also kind of annoyed in the same breath since she interrupted an important thought I was about to jot down.

"Your soap opera?" she says innocently.

Now I really look at her, her hair the same color as Adeline and mine, passed down from generations of Reeses. She has Brad's eyes, a dark, crystalline blue, and when she gets a little bit older, she'll be making those boys crawl at her ankles.

"I don't write a soap. Who told you that?" Because eleven-year-olds don't typically know what that is.

"Uncle Noah, he said your job was to write drama for a fake soap opera."

I have to chuckle at this, because it's so Noah. He's not even saying it to be mean, more likely he really doesn't know what I do on a daily basis and was blowing the kids off with a simple answer.

"Well, Uncle Noah is wrong. I write for a primetime drama, which is light-years better than a soap opera. Don't tell anyone I said that, though. Would make me look bad." I wink at her.

"I won't tell." She pretends to lock her mouth with a key. "Can I help?"

Oh, crap. She thinks this is some kind of homework assignment, not the ever-important work of furthering a romantic storyline in subtle glances and layered dialogue between characters.

"It's actually probably best if I just—"

I'm about to tell her to go play on her own, or do whatever eleven-year-olds do these days, but then I catch her eyes. She's got a hunger in them, more than I saw in even myself at her age. Delilah wants a taste of the outside world, the universe outside of Texas and her family bubble.

And I'll be damned if she doesn't remind me a lot of myself.

I'm stuck at her house tonight because Adeline and Brad wanted to have a date night, and their babysitter suddenly canceled. I'm not sure if that actually happened, or if it was just an excuse to make me spend time with my niece and nephews. I'm thinking the latter, but I have no proof.

Not that I'm complaining. I came over and heated up the spaghetti casserole Adeline left for us, and sat down at the table with Delilah and her twin brothers, Max and Michael. The three of them were surprisingly funny, for kids under the age of puberty. Max and Michael got into a heated discussion about if dinosaurs were real, and it was rousing dinner table conversation. Delilah told me a story about the time Adeline accidentally locked the three kids in the car, and I not only laughed until my stomach hurt, but it made me feel a little better knowing my sister wasn't one hundred percent perfect.

Then we'd washed up, gotten them in pajamas, and brushed their teeth, and put the twins to bed. I have to say, playing auntie is fun. The kids make me laugh, gave me a few tastes of my own medicine from when I was a child, and the unconditional love they feel for me even though I haven't fully been in their lives is amazing.

At first, I didn't want to get to know any of them. I knew it would make it harder to go back to New York. And my assumption was completely correct. I've only spent a couple of hours with Adeline's brood, and they're already attaching themselves to my heart.

Case in point, I'm allowing Delilah to stay up an extra hour after the twins, a lie I'm pretty sure she thinks fooled me when she said her mom lets her do it all the time.

"Let me just finish up this scene, and then I'll let you help me with the next one, okay?" I tell her, passing the bowl of chocolate chips and popcorn I threw together as a writing snack.

This little girl does not need to be involved in the writing of a sex scene, of that I'm sure. Her mother would kill me.

It takes me another twenty minutes to hash out the scene, input the dialogue, and then give it my seal of approval. Hopefully, Donna will be happy with it. I've had another two phone calls with her in the week and half I've been staying down here, and they've been productive. But I can tell she's not sold on the arrangement, and I know that anyone in the show business arena is replaceable. Even a writer as good as I know I am—they'll find someone to do it cheaper and faster.

My fingers go to my lips as I write the last word of the sex scene, and damn him to hell, I can still taste Jason on them days later.

Why did he have to go and kiss me? I was so furious at him

for bringing my mother up again, for pushing into concrete boundaries I'd set long ago. Jason was trying to address old wounds, ones I never wanted to talk about again.

And then he'd gone and broken all the rules, taking something that was off-limits to him now. And I'd been stupid enough to match him, kiss for kiss.

But lord, did it feel like I was alive for the first time in ten years. Like I'd been a caged bird, kept from the light for a decade, and he was finally opening the door. The feel of his mouth on mine, the connection that ran between us like pulsing electrical currents, it shocked my heart into beating the correct way for the first time since I'd left Hale.

I hated him for that. For showing me that my prim, proper little life back in New York was nothing compared to what we had. I also hate myself for still thinking about the kiss. For wanting to do it again. For keeping it from Perry, because what am I supposed to tell him about my high school sweetheart he doesn't even know exists?

Guilt and frustration are just a constant sickness in my gut these days, and if I don't deal with it, I'm going to explode.

"Can I help now?" Delilah interrupts my thoughts.

Shaking my head, I plaster on a smile. "Yes. Okay, so I'm going to start a scene about a new patient coming into the hospital. Basically, the show I write for is about a bunch of doctors who work as surgeons, and how their patients and cases affect them."

Delilah nods her head, biting on her lip as if she's thinking. "What if we wrote about this girl in my class? She and her family went on a cruise to the Bahamas, and when she came back, they found out she had an actual fish living in her stomach!"

And just like that, I realize my niece has more of a mind for this than I ever thought she could. I assumed she'd come up with some childish idea that I'd have to morph, or just change later, but this was actually interesting.

"Gross." We giggle together, and then I ask, "How did she get it?"

"She and her cousin, who was on the cruise, were in a truth or dare battle. Her cousin dared her to swallow the fish while her family was snorkeling, so she did it. She thought she'd just poop it out!"

That has us laughing again, and I start to type, the scene coming alive in my head. "Okay, I'm going to have her parents rush her in, and then the whole family will come running in behind her like ... you know the airport scene in *Home Alone*?"

Delilah nods. "Of course! They're all running around like crazy people!"

I point at her. "Exactly! It'll be chaos, and then the actress who will play your friend will be real quiet. Then she'll barf on one of the doctor's shoes."

She cackles, and I know she sees the scene, too. "And then she can yell at her cousin. Maybe she can say something like 'I wish I made you eat that starfish!'"

It's actually pretty funny, and on brand to the scene, so I put it in. We spend about twenty more minutes plotting the scene together and creating dialogue, and then I have to bribe Delilah up to bed with another chocolate chip cookie from the jar on the top shelf of the pantry.

Hanging out with my niece, hearing her thoughts and seeing the world through her eyes, it's been one of the best highlights of my year.

Hours later, after the kids are asleep and I'm basically seeing tunnel-vision at the contracts and scripts I'm looking through, the lock on the front door clicks. Adeline and Brad quietly walk into the living room, goofy smiles on their faces. It's kind of refreshing to see how in love they are, even after all these years.

"Hey, thanks for getting them to bed. Did they give you much trouble?" she asks, sitting down beside my pile of papers.

I shake my head, glancing over at her. "Not at all. They're good kids, Addy. It was nice to spend some time with them."

Her hands reach out, twisting a lock of my hair in a motherly fashion. "I'm worried you're working yourself into the ground."

Chuckling, I tell her the truth. "If I don't, someone else who will, will just come along and take my job. It's a grind. At home, I spend about sixty to seventy hours a week working. Perry works even longer hours than I do."

And unlike my friends in Manhattan, who all compete to see who works the longest and can resist the burn out, Adeline frowns.

"That's not something to brag about, Savvy. You're an excellent storyteller, we've all always known that. But if this is just a glimpse into your life, it makes me sad. You're so young, so much younger than you think. You should be traveling and falling in love with everything around you. Thinking about your life ahead, and how you want to fill it with joy. Does this give you joy? Does Perry working eighty-hour weeks give you joy?"

If I needed any confirmation that my siblings were pulling for me to fall back in love with Jason while I was here, this was it.

"So, what you're implying is that I need to come back to Hale and end up in Jason Whitney's bed to be happy?" I raise an eyebrow at her.

Adeline has the decency to blush. "That's not what I'm saying, although it is my wildest hope. But no, what I want for you is a life full of meaningful relationships and soul-deep happiness. I may have days where I want to rip my hair out and scream at my children, or bitch at my husband for leaving dirty dishes in the sink, but at the end of the day, I'm so happy. There is no other life I'd rather be living."

"How do you know? You don't see me in my life," I fire back.

She sighs, swiping a thumb across my jaw like Mom used to do to all of us. "Because, Savannah, I remember the light that used to shine in my little sister's eyes, and I don't see that at all anymore. You may be content, secure, but you're not happy. Whether it's here or there, with your Perry or alone or with someone entirely new ... I, *we*, just want you to be happy."

Adeline rises from the couch. "Anyways, I'm glad you were able to spend time with the kids. They were really excited about it. We've missed you."

She disappears into another room, or maybe upstairs with Brad, leaving me to let myself out.

Why is it that I can step foot back in this freaking town and question everything about myself?

Because these people are your mirrors, and they'll always show you the things you're avoiding looking at, the little voice whispers in my ear, and in the back of my mind, I know it's true.

Family is always going to know you best, even if you want to hate them for it.

17

JASON

The chips clank against the table, cards shuffling in our hands.

We all tell each other that this is just a friendly game of poker, that it's just a night for guy friends to get together, but we're all bullshit liars. Each one of us has about two beers and a competitive streak gnawing at our guts. It's all for bragging rights and chump change, no one ever wins anything significant. But to claim the twenty-dollar pot and talk up our ego around town until the next poker night, we all become teenage boys comparing our junk sizes.

Noah, Jenks, Beau, and I sit around the table that Jenks purchased at a yard sale over two years ago. It smells like cigarettes and mothballs, but playing on an actual poker table is better than playing on a folding table in Beau's garage, so here we are.

"Deal 'em," I tell Jenks, who has been shuffling the cards needlessly for five minutes now.

"You just want to redeem yourself. Folding the first two rounds? Rookie move, Jay," Beau taunts me.

"I'm not giving you assholes my quarters over shit hands." I flip him off.

Noah takes a sip of beer. "Per usual, Jay won't give in to anything that won't go his way."

He's goading me, has been all night, and we both know it ain't about poker. He's pissed that I'm making no headway with his sister, but little does he know that I attacked her mouth the other night with mine.

And ever since, she's been avoiding me.

We haven't worked on the house in three days, and I haven't seen Savannah anywhere. She's either holed up inside the apartment above Rudy's, since I heard she'd been renting it, or somewhere else, because Hale isn't big enough for me to not run into her.

And I wasn't going to work on the house without her. It was my mission to keep her in Hale as long as possible, not book her plane ticket back to New York.

Plus, I've been out at the winery quite a lot. Shit, I slept on the couch in my office two nights ago because I was so busy making up the posters and menus for opening weekend next week. It's officially April in Texas, which means the weather goes from rainy and bipolar to a hundred degrees in the span of a nightfall. We've been cleaning out the tasting rooms, setting up the tent in the back vineyard, pulling the tables and chairs from storage and just putting every finishing touch on things.

And by we, I mean me and my very short list of staff members. I only have four full timers, one sommelier, two cooks, my customer service/everything else crisis handler, and the lead guest experience manager who runs the tasting room. The rest of my help is part-time or seasonal.

We're kicking off opening weekend with a huge festival; a full lineup of bands, sale on all of our wines, two private parties thrown in there, and a special six-course dinner that is pay-ahead and limited to fifty people.

I also may be avoiding thinking of any of my personal shit going on, which is why I've been working myself to the bone. Sleep hasn't come easy, and when it does, I only dream of Savannah and that kiss. Of her saying things to me that she will never say again.

So work it is.

We play a hand, which I lose again, and then Jenks goes over to his basement fridge to replenish our beers.

"Did I tell you guys that Nancy wants another baby?" Jenks pops the tops with a bottle opener and hands them out.

"Another? You've got three already!" I exclaim, befuddled.

Jenks shrugs. "But they're all so dang cute. She said four would even us out perfectly."

"Or put you in a mental institution." Beau shakes his head. "I only have two and I have no idea how you handle a brood that outnumbers you."

"It's chaos, but it's kind of nice. Like some days, I think my brain is going to fall out of my ears because one of them has asked me about sixty thousand questions, but then they hug me and it's totally worth it."

Noah smiles, sipping from his beer. "I know what you mean. Hope wants about six more, and I'm like 'who is going to pay for all of these kids,' but I don't really care either. The love, man ... it's unlike anything else."

"You're all suckers." I chuckle.

Though, I'd like kids of my own someday. I always thought it would happen sometime down the line, when I was with Savannah, but the older I get, the more I realize that the "down the line" time is *now*. I'm thirty, and not getting any younger, and I have this dream of being able to throw a baseball around with my son.

"You seen Sav this week?" Noah asks.

His voice is casual, but I know this conversation is about to be anything but.

I shrug, doing this non-committal noise.

"That's a yes, then." Jenks snorts, dealing the cards.

"She's only been here two weeks, and I found him whistling in The Whistlestop the other day." Beau rolls his eyes.

"So, you've slept together, then." Jenks surmises.

I cough, sputtering over my beer. "Dude, seriously? Noah is sitting right there."

Noah gives Jenks a disgusted look. "That's my sister."

"Plus, not that it's any of your business, but no, we haven't. She has a boyfriend. And I ... I don't know that I want her back."

They all start cackling. It's a good thing I didn't tell them about the kiss, because then my last sentence would sound even more pathetic.

"We all know that's a lie. But aside from that, she just seems so different, man." Noah shakes his head.

"We're all different," Jenks agrees.

Beau snorts. "You still have the same hat you wore in middle school, and won't drive down the street that flooded on your eighth birthday 'cause you're still pissed at it."

Jenks shoots him a glaring look. "Screw off. I don't like change."

"None of us do, it's why we live in the same sleepy town we grew up in," I say.

"Says the guy who has ordered thousand-dollar parts for his beat-up old trucks instead of junking that old heap and getting a new one." Noah chuckles under his breath.

I wag my finger at him. "Don't you go insulting Betsy, now."

"Yeah, that's the man's truck. And we won't get started on how you won't marry Hope because you think it'll change something. Talk about afraid of change." Jenks raises an eyebrow in his direction.

Noah rolls his eyes at the sheriff. "Whatever. All I'm saying is, no one seems to be able to figure her out. She is ... cold. Which I'm not used to with Savannah. She used to be the most compassionate of us all. She was the storyteller, the one who'd grill you for every detail and try to mend the broken hearts or souls. And sometimes I see little glimpses of that, but then she tucks it back away."

"Would you be okay if what happened to her happened to you?" Jenks asks in all seriousness.

We all look at him, a little surprised he's taking up for Savvy.

"What?" He looks incredulous. "First, her childhood sweetheart loses everything they've both been working toward, and she's forced to become a nurse overnight. I love you, Jay, but you were a cold-hearted bastard those months after your injury. And then, just as she's coping with your dream going down the drain, her mother passes. Sorry, Noah, no offense meant. It's just ... I could see why she bolted."

We're all quiet for a minute, and then Noah pipes up. "Honestly, I never thought about it that way, but you're kind of right. It's a lot for anyone to handle, much less an eighteen-year-old girl."

"If you're telling me it's my fault, I already know that," I grumble.

Beau shakes his head. "No one is saying that. We're just looking at it from the other side."

I swing my head his way, my jaw almost unhinging, but Noah beats me to it. "Hold on just one damn minute. Are you telling me that you're siding with my sister? After all these years of cursing her name and threatening mutiny if she ever came back, you suddenly see her point?"

"I'm a rational man, I could see how difficult that could be.

Plus, I've got daughters now. I'd want them to heal for as long as they needed if something that tragic happened to them."

I've spent a lot of time mad at myself, mad at the world, and mad at Savannah. Shit, I probably eat the emotion fury for breakfast. In the last ten years, I've become sullen, ground down my molars, and rarely smile if it's not for someone I truly love and appreciate.

Maybe the guys are right. Maybe it's time to let this all go, to sit Savvy down and really listen to her. Without defensiveness, without my own bruised ego, there could be a discussion and a way to move on.

Even though I told them I didn't know if I wanted her back, they could see through it in seconds.

If there was a way that she and I could forgive our past, then I could make one last-ditch effort to show her that she belongs with me.

18

SAVANNAH

A knock sounds at the door just as I'm finishing a round of emails to the editing staff on continuity, direction, and overall arch of the episodes I've written.

People think my job ends at just penning the story for the show, but in reality, I'm behind the scenes twenty-four seven making sure that my brainchild goes off without a hitch. If I get video playbacks of the scenes and I don't like how the actors portrayed it, I'm going to say something. Of course, this is much harder being in Texas rather than on location in New York, because everything is delayed.

It's only a few more weeks, I have to keep reminding myself. Although, who knows. I've almost been here for a month now, and in the last week, Jason and I have done nothing on the house. I haven't even been out there. I'm so afraid to face it, to face him, after our fight and the kiss. It's going to be so stiflingly awkward and forced, and he might try to talk to me about it when all I want to do is ignore the fact it ever happened.

So, we're at a standoff, and I have no clue whether he's been out there to fix it up. Although, why would he do that? He's the one who let it fall into disrepair for years, for God knows what reason. So, if it isn't my acceleration of the project, it's not like he'd go out there to work on it.

My white fluffy open-toed slippers shuffle across the floor of my makeshift apartment as I go to answer the door.

Cecily stands there, bright and cheery in a yellow sundress, two hulking books in her hands.

"Hey!" She bends to kiss my cheek, and I smile, because she's just ... so herself.

We've bumped into each other in town a few more times, and she always says we should get together. The sentiment is nice, but I just ... I don't know how to be around my old friends here. I feel like I'm living an out-of-body experience, like basic human functions are hard to do. I feel like an actor, walking around focusing too hard on what my arms are doing instead of just being natural.

It's not that I don't want to open up, to smile and laugh with them, I just feel like an alien.

"Hey, how are you? What time ... isn't it a workday?" I ask, moving to check my wrist and realizing I haven't put my watch on.

Now that I think about it, I haven't put my watch on in a couple of days. It's one of the electronic ones that pairs with my phone, so I get all of my updates and notifications no matter where I go. But since I've been here, I've been disconnecting, and it feels ...

Spectacular.

I didn't even realize I was falling into the slow way of life that Texas exudes until right this minute.

"Hank said I could knock off early, we don't have many patients today."

Cecily works as the receptionist for the only doctor in town. Hank Wright works out of an old Victorian house, and the bedrooms are his patient rooms. Ceci keeps his schedule, acts as a nurse sometimes, and generally keeps the whole operation legally running.

"Oh, okay. Um, come on in." I invite her in to my temporary home.

Even though I wasn't thrilled at the prospect of living above Rudy's when I have a three-thousand-foot penthouse waiting for me in Manhattan, I've kind of come to love this place. It's cozy and smells of coffee at all times. It's a solitary space with exposed brick and just enough nostalgia creeping in at its corners to keep me inspired at all times. This apartment is the perfect writer's nook, and I won't lie and say I won't miss it when I go.

"Can I get you a drink? What are those?" I ask, pointing to the pile in her arms.

"I'll take some sweet tea, if you have some." She knows I do. It's the first thing I stocked up on at the grocery store, because they just don't make it like the same on the East Coast.

Taking two mismatched glasses from the cabinet above the small stove, I fill them with ice and cool amber tea.

"I brought our old yearbooks," she says giddily from behind me.

When I turn, I find her seated on the floor between the couch and the coffee table; the books laid out in front of her.

Too curious to be annoyed at revisiting the past, I grab the drinks and make my way to her.

"Oh my God, where did you find these?" I marvel, looking at the dusty covers.

"I dug them out of the basement. It's been a while since I looked at them, and I just thought, what the hell. You coming back here has made me so reminiscent of the old days. Our glory days!" She claps her hands like the cheerleader she once was.

Folding myself so I can sit next to her, I hand her the tea as she thumbs through the pages.

"Stop!" I say, spotting a familiar picture.

It's from our junior year, and Cecily stands next to my locker in her cheer uniform. I'm leaning on the other side, glancing up at Jason with practically heart shapes for my eyes. Around us are our friends, people from the baseball team, or my student council government buddies. We're all laughing; the kind of expressions that only teenagers with no adult responsibilities could have.

"Gosh, we all look so young." She breathes, tracing our faces. "If I could only still fit into that uniform, Thomas would have a field day."

That makes me snicker. "What else is in here?"

We flip through the pages together, laughing at our cheesy headshots, and my braces phase, which was just ending junior year. We find Cecily's cheerleading picture as a co-captain, and a picture of us hugging in front of the pep rally banner.

Then we come across the one picture I've looked at dozens of times.

"Aw, will you look at that." Ceci sighs dreamily.

It's a huge square photo at the top right of the page, the one marked "junior prom." I'm in the special pink glittery dress Mama took me all the way to Abilene to pick out, my hair piled on my head in curls. Around my wrist is a matching pink corsage, and my smile couldn't stretch any wider if I'd tried.

Because ... I'm in Jason's arms. His face is still boyish in the picture, compared to the man I've encountered now, and he's in his rented black tux that gapped on his still-developing frame.

And he's looking down at me, during that slow dance to "Halo" by Beyoncé, as if I painted the whole night's sky. We're looking at each other like two people who could power the world's energy with our love.

"We sure were happy, huh?" I don't catch myself before I blurt it out.

"Everyone used to want to be you two. I just wanted y'all to adopt me." Cecily rubs my shoulder.

"Sometimes, I wish I could go back to that moment in time, when everything was perfect."

"Was it, though? I mean, you still had braces, and sex hadn't even gotten good yet." She laughs, and I join her.

"You're right. That was saved for senior year." I can't help but bite my tongue at the hilarious image of Jason and I losing it to each other.

We had no idea what we were doing, and it showed. Eventually, awful became decent, decent became good, and good became phenomenal. We practiced a lot.

Cecily pulls the other book in front of us. "Then I guess we're ready for this."

Together, we flip the pages of our senior yearbook, laughing at the memories and hilarious pictures of classmates. We find her senior picture, beautiful in her grandmother's pearls with that black cape they put on you. Then comes mine, with my mother's locket around my neck. I reach up, realizing I left that locket buried in some jewelry chest back in New York. I'll have to pull it out when I go back.

The quote under my picture is what gets me.

Some things tie your life together, slender threads and things to treasure.

Days like that should last and last and last.

They're lyrics from the song "Dusk and Summer" by Dashboard Confessional, off the album that defined my senior year into the summer that defined us forever.

The melody of that song plays in my mind now, a heartbreaking summer ballad that reminds me of sunsets and tall grass and sneaking out and drinking on the field behind Cecily's family farm.

"We really did live the life then, huh?" I bump her shoulder with mine.

She takes a sip of tea. "They were the best of times. But we can have more, ya know."

"Oh, yeah?" I know she has an idea on the brain.

Ceci jumps up like an agile jaguar.

"Come on, you need a nice, relaxing day at the salon." She pulls at my arm.

"Oh, no you don't." I back up, trying to escape her.

"Savvy, you deserve it! You've been cooped up in here for a week, and your nails look like a wreck." She blinks down at my hands.

Defensively, I pull my hands back. "How rude!"

She shrugs. "Just being honest. And you know that these girls are already gossiping about you. Imagine if they saw those cuticles."

The sparkle in her eye is the only thing that makes me smile. Because what she's proposing is a social suicide bomber mission. I'll be walking right into the belly of the beast going to the salon.

"If even one of them makes a comment about my Yankee hairstyle or lack of hairspray ..." I point a finger at her.

Cecily loops her arm through mine, barely giving me time to change out of my slippers.

"Don't worry, I'll block the busy bees and their stingers. This is going to be fun!"

19

SAVANNAH

We walk into Stacy's Salon, which is basically just like every other southern hair salon you've ever imagined. If you picture Truvy's in the movie *Steel Magnolias*, then you're pretty much ninety percent of the way there.

Stacy McManus has owned the salon for nearly thirty years, almost as long as I've been alive. According to Facebook and Cecily, two girls who dropped out of our high school class and went to cosmetology school currently work there, as well as Bertha and Janice, the two stylists who are as much of a staple as Stacy.

I remember coming in here every third Saturday with my mama, so she could get her roots dyed. My sisters and I would ask for manicures for every birthday or special event, and Cecily and I practically grew up on Stacy's swing set in the backyard. Our mothers would gather with the other local moms to gossip, drink tea, and get beautified.

And apparently, it's the same thing that happened on a random Thursday nowadays, as well.

"I wondered when you'd be by to see me!"

Stacy comes barreling at me, her large chest almost bouncing out of the tank top she's sporting. She engulfs me in a bear hug, and my initial shock dissolves into a warm comfort. She's of my mother's era, and something about her embrace has me struggling through the grief I feel for Mama every day.

Clearing my throat, I back out of the hug. "You were on my list of must-see stops."

"And it's a good thing, too. Your ends are dry as a Texas summer, sweetheart." She picks at my hair even though I've given her no permission.

I shoot a death glare at Cecily, who shrugs, because we're only five seconds in and already there have been comments about my hair.

"We're just here for manicures, Stac. Hi y'all!" Cecily wags her fingers at the stylists and all the women in the salon.

I recognize ... well, everyone. Jenks wife, Nancy, who we went to high school with, sits in Bertha's chair. And then there is Kaitlyn Meyers, Olivia Bloom, and Franny Welden. All girls we went to school with, who were in our friend group, and are actively looking me up and down. I feel the judgment swirling, the gossip gathering behind their tongues, and for a moment, I'm terrified.

And then I remember who I am. Then it all becomes entertainment and pastime. Gossiping in the salon is a southern pastime, one I forgot I loved. In New York, I plug my headphones in whenever I get my hair or nails done, and barely make eye contact with the person working on me.

"All right, loves, choose your colors and then sit at those stations," Stacy instructs us.

Cecily goes with bright Barbie pink, while I pick a mauve-gray that has no business in the kind of weather Texas is bringing right now.

We sit down next to each other, and without a word, Stacy brings us over two cold glasses of tea.

And before I even get my hands in the bowl of soaking water, they start up.

"Did you see what Hannah was wearing at church last weekend?" Nancy says.

"Someone could have seen straight up to her cooter when she went for communion. Nicholas really needs to teach her what's what," Olivia agrees.

"Who is Hannah?" I ask Cecily.

Kaitlyn cuts her off. "Remember Nicholas, the outfielder on the baseball team our senior year?"

I nod, vaguely remembering his face.

"Well, he married this girl named Hannah from Chile, we suspect because she was pregnant. But there was never any baby, and now he's locked in. Anyways, she's a typical Chile girl."

Stacy and Janice sit down across from us, prepping our cuticles and nail beds. The massage Janice is working over my fingers feels heavenly, and I'm glad I let Ceci talk me into this.

The rest of the salon snickers, because we all know what it means to be a Chile girl. The town over was, for lack of a better term, trash. A lot of drugs, a lot of unemployment, and the people there were a product of their environment. It wasn't nice, the way they were patronizing a girl from Chile, but I could only imagine the outfit she'd worn to church.

"If it wasn't her ass, it was her boobs hanging out. I swear, I almost had to take my Jimmy out of that church." Nancy scoffs, and I still can't believe that people I graduated with have kids that are of the age of noticing a woman's curves.

"Are y'all going to the vineyard opening weekend?" Cecily asks, joining in on the local newswire.

"Wouldn't miss it. A night of getting drunk without my kids? I'm in." Olivia giggles.

"Jason does such a good job. I just can't wait to have some of that Tex Mex they bring in from Austin. I've been craving that street corn they make. Oh crap, I might be pregnant again," Kaitlyn whines.

His name registers in my brain, but I keep my mouth shut. I want to know what the opening of the vineyard is about, and how Jason is involved. Maybe I can ask Cecily later, but it's shark bait opening my mouth in here. Once I show interest in my ex-boyfriend, they're all going to pounce.

Stacy rumbles a laugh. "You and Landry really don't take no breaks do you?"

"The man is a fiend. I gotta get me some birth control."

Olivia gasps. "Don't even joke."

I can't stop from rolling my eyes, and Cecily swallows a snort next to me. Here we are, gossiping about everyone in the entire town's vaginas, but these women think going on the pill is ungodly. If they only knew the two times I ran to CVS down my block to buy Plan B.

Two seconds later, they're onto the next subject. We spend the entire rest of the afternoon, long after our nails dry, just chatting at the salon.

By the time Cecily drops me off back at my apartment, I feel in tune with the girl I used to be.

Dropping my head back against the headrest, I smile over at Ceci. "Thank you for today. It was ... entertaining."

"My pleasure. Now your nails and your ears are up to Hale standards."

"Ears?" I raise an eyebrow.

"Don't pretend you weren't engrossed in that story about Mrs. Jires having an affair with her next-door neighbor."

"You caught me." I chuckle. "It was too good not to ask about the entire situation."

"She's still in there, you know," Cecily says.

"Huh?" I'm confused.

"The girl you used to be. I love seeing this strong woman you've become, but that wild, carefree girl is still in there, too. I know you're doubting that. I had a hard time letting some of that side of me go as well. I'm sure it's been harder for you to be back here because everything feels foreign. But I can still see that love you have for everyone here. You can take the girl out of Texas, but you can't take Texas out of the girl."

My old best friend winks at me, and I feel so much relief that I want to cry.

Wiping at my eyes, which are getting misty, I reach out to grab her hand.

"I thought I knew who I was. For the last ten years, I've had this identity that I thought could not be tested. I've been strong, and self-sufficient. I'm used to doing things on my own, or closing myself off if things get too scary in terms of emotions. The minute I stepped foot back here, it was like all the concrete I thought I was standing on turned into quicksand."

Cecily nods, chewing on her lip as her own eyes get misty.

"Maybe it's a good thing, you know? Going through this test. You showed me today that I can still be her, the girl I came from. My roots are still in here," I rub my chest over my heart, "but my wings are, too. I can combine them, take the best of both and become the person I was always meant to be. How is it that I'm almost thirty and still questioning who I am?"

My friend smiles wistfully. "I think that if we're not questioning ourselves every single day, we're not really alive. You don't have to know who you are, not now, and not when you're fifty. Hell, you could pick up some random activity some day when you're forty-seven, like hiking every mountain trail in the continental United States!"

We both giggle, because me doing any kind of voluntary physical outdoor activity is laughable.

"But you could, and it might be the thing you realize you were put on this earth for. People find their calling at all different times. It's not really about that. I guess we just have to take each day as a new opportunity to live fiercely and love without regret."

My voice is a whisper as it comes out. "Since when did you get so smart?"

"Been reading a lot of Oprah." She giggles, and we break into a fit of laughter.

The day leaves me with even more questions, but a sense of peace I didn't know I was searching for.

20

SAVANNAH

After my trip to the salon, and sit-down dinner with my family, I begin to settle into the routine of Hale like I haven't in the weeks I've been here.

I start to work down in The Whistlestop, chatting with Rudy or anyone who wanders in. I go to church for the first Sunday in more than ten years, and take Cecily out to dinner at Buddy's, even though she puts it on the family tab. We get too tipsy on margaritas and then end up joking about going cow tipping. Stacy wrangles me into a knitting circle one night, and I think of Mama the entire time. Adeline gets our mother's spare yarn out of her attic, and I make a little doll's outfit for one of Noah's girls.

The South has been injected back into me, and I slow way down. Being on my own, in the apartment, is something I relish. I've been out to the house twice, to finish the painting, and don't see Jason at all. But I don't mind. I'm having a love affair with my hometown and remembering all the parts of me that I'd long ago abandoned.

Before I know it, another week passes, and Perry is on me about what the hell I'm doing down here.

"You need to get back here. They're threatening to call the backup buyers." His voice is angry and short.

Stepping out of Gilo's, the Mexican restaurant in Hale, I cover the receiver with my hand. No one on the street knows who I'm talking to, but internally, I'm embarrassed. My boyfriend is currently talking to me like I'm a petulant child.

"I'm trying, Perry. Things here are more complicated than I thought. And if they're that insistent, let them call the backups. There are hundreds of nice apartments in Manhattan, we'll find one."

I think I actually hear him choke on something on the other end of the phone. "You're serious right now? What the hell are you talking about, Savannah? We have been waiting almost a year on this specific apartment, it's the cornerstone in our plan. It hits every item on our checklist; his and her bathrooms, Italian marble countertops, a multi-thousand-dollar security system. And now you're just willing to let it go? What the hell has gotten into you?"

As he lists off all the things I thought were important just months ago, I'm kind of disgusted. Did we really need two separate bathrooms? Wasn't the point of moving in with your significant other to share all spaces, to get to know each other on an intimate level?

But his other point has my palms sweating. I was fixated on getting the penthouse. In fact, it was my number one goal this year; there had been nothing else more important to me. Hell, I'd gone down to Hale like a bat out of hell just to set my credit straight so we could snag the penthouse.

There was just no fight left in me for it. In fact, I felt more at home in the small apartment above Rudy's shop than I knew I ever would in the glass and marble monstrosity we'd been bidding on. I'm not sure when that changed, but it just had. And I couldn't deny it now.

I didn't even know I was questioning anything until I got here. Part of me wishes I never came here, that I resolved it all from New York. The other part of me realizes that I could have had a complete breakdown four months from now when I moved into an apartment with Perry and finally had to face the fears and doubts that had been lying dormant for so long.

"I just ... coming down here showed me that some things are just different. We felt a lot of pressure on this property anyway, and the board was so stuffy and judgmental. I'll get things settled here, and we'll take our time finding a place that really is our own," I try to reassure him.

Silence greets my positive spin for a few moments.

"That was the perfect place, and now we're going to lose it. Because what? You went back to Oklahoma? This isn't you, Savannah." Perry never called me by a nickname.

His lack of knowledge on me, or listening skills when I said where I was flying home to, wounds me. I guess it's partly my fault; I've never told Perry much of anything about my childhood or why I came to New York. I never wanted to discuss it, and he never asked. It was like my life started over completely when I moved to Manhattan, and that's the only version of me he wanted to know.

"I'm in Texas," I mutter, knowing he won't care.

"Fine, Texas." Perry is quiet for a second. "I feel like I'm losing you."

And then my heart fractures a little. Because I'm throwing our life for a loop. He's been so good to me, and we've really built something together. What I'm doing isn't fair to Perry; he's done nothing but try to make my dreams come true. And I'm not even trying to accurately explain to him why I'm having this change of heart about so many things. This man loves me, and I love him.

Not to mention keeping a gigantic secret about kissing Jason the other week. I'll never tell him that, because it won't happen again and there is no purpose in mentioning it.

"I'm so sorry, Per. I don't mean to be vague or short, it's just that I've reconnected with an old part of myself down here and it's opening my eyes to some things. You knew how broken I was when you met me, and part of that is about what happened here. You're not losing me. I promise, I'll be done here soon and then I'm coming back to you."

There is a sigh of relief on the other end. "Good, I miss you terribly. Just ... get it done, okay? In the meantime, I'll start apartment hunting again."

We hang up with mutual I love you's, and then I know what I have to do.

I haven't been working on the house, keeping up my end of the deal with Perry. It's time to, like he said, *get it done*. So, I head out, fully intending on spending the rest of the day fixing up as much as I can.

When I pull up to the house, it's such a muggy day and I'm so frustrated that I don't even go inside. I bypass it, heading for the back of the house. My sandals trudge through the overgrown lawn and weeds as big as trees, a problem Jason will have to address if he puts this place on the market. But finally, I get through it, and the sparkle of the crystalline water instantly soothes my soul.

The hills form on all sides, creating a valley filled with a large lake. It's so big that you can't even see the other end, and it's what spurred us to buy the shack off Jason's uncle. I imagined summers here, wading into the lake, spending nights skinny dipping in it.

This lake has always been a source of comfort to me; after my mother's funeral, I came here to be alone. I sat on the shabby dock and put my toes in the water, letting the salt of my tears mix with the inky black water.

And so I come here now. When nothing feels solid under my feet, I know it's where I need to go. My life is in upheaval, nothing I thought would hold true is really doing so, and I don't feel like addressing it. Shedding my jeans and shoes, I leave my cell phone and keys on top of the pile on shore.

The minute the water hits my ankles, I'm overcome with this intense feeling of peace. I think my parents might be here with me right now, in this spot, looking over me. My head sinks under and I swim, stroking through the water as a distraction to every problem plaguing me. I dive down, trying to touch the bottom, but fail and scurry back up.

When I break the surface, the sun sparkles in my eyes, and I take lungfuls of breath. There is no noise out here except for the birds high up in the trees, and it's the quietest place I've been in many years.

"Didn't anyone ever tell you, you're not supposed to swim alone?" Jason's voice comes from the dock.

"I think you remember how good of a swimmer I am. I'd save myself," I tell him, no malice in my voice.

As I float on my back, wet T-shirt sticking to my breasts and my underwear in full view of him to see, I no longer care. Even though the root of all my problems is standing on the shores, the water is keeping me at peace right now. I'm not going to let the anger or sadness in.

"Do you have some sixth sense about when I'm at this house?" I ask, because it's happened so many times now.

I hear a quiet lapping of water and assume that he's sitting with his feet off the dock. We used to do this a lot, me swimming and him watching.

"I haven't been out in a few days, wanted to come see if a bear had decimated it or not."

That makes me laugh. "Why the heck, after ten years of this

craphole still impossibly standing, would a bear come out and knock it down after we actually put some work into it?"

Jason fires back with quick wit. "It's all that vanilla perfume you wear. They can probably smell it from a mile away, come running thinking some idiots left cookies or ice cream out."

"Ah, so now these bears have a sweet tooth and a penchant for womanly fragrances?"

"It's not up to me what those bears decide to like."

We both chuckle over the ridiculous conversation, and I finally bob upright, looking at him. He's in khaki shorts and a plain white T-shirt, the muscles of his biceps and pecs straining against the material. There are dirt streaks on it, and one down his right cheek. His midnight-black hair is tousled, like he's been pulling at it all day.

And Jesus, does he look good enough to eat. The kiss we shared lingers between us, neither of us daring to pick up that hot potato. Slowly, Jason takes the hem of his shirt and slides it up, each inch of skin revealed burning in my memory. It's agonizing and forbidden, I shouldn't be looking and he shouldn't be doing this.

Yet, here we are.

After he's done, he sets aside the items in his pockets, and then slides into the water. It's like a commercial for something vague; cologne or fast cars or hair gel. Unnecessarily sexy, and yet you want to know what the advertisement is selling.

Jason sinks under, and then comes up, wiping water from his perfect bone structure.

"Remember when you thought there was an eel in here?" He grins.

And now that he says it, I squirm, swimming in circles. "I swear, I felt it shock me."

"It was definitely just a piece of seaweed." That devilish smile is too close, swimming circles around me like a shark.

It occurs to me that in the time I've been back in Hale, we haven't had one conversation that isn't laced with tension or us screaming at each other.

"Has time been kind to you, Jason?" I ask, genuinely curious.

He looks surprised. "What?"

"Do you like your life? Are you happy?" As much as I hate him for what went down all those years ago, I ... I've never wanted him to suffer.

That gorgeous face tilts to the side as he treads water.

"Yeah, I guess I am happy. As happy as a guy could be in my position. My life is better than it was when I was growing up; I'm not waiting around for a family that doesn't want me or have the drama of where I'm getting my next meal. I have friends who care about me, a house, a job. It's not what I thought I'd be doing, but I try not to wonder what life would have looked like now if I hadn't gotten hurt. One lesson I've learned very well is not to dwell too much on what didn't happen. Well, in some cases."

His words echo in my head. *You don't love him, don't you feel this?*

Of course, I felt it. I still feel it. Not feeling the attraction, the chemistry, the love between us? You'd have to be a robot, or a cyborg, or something like one of those science fiction plots that Donna is always trying to shove at me. They have no business on a medical show, and I have no business exploring the very real feelings that still exist between Jason and me.

But if that was a lesson he hadn't learned when it came to us, I had to admit I hadn't either. There were nights, more than I'd like to own up to, where I'd lie awake and wonder if this was it. If Perry and New York were what my destiny held. And then my mind would wander back to the rolling plains of Texas and Jason. I'd envision what our life would have been, how old our kids would be. I pictured us sitting in Adirondack chairs on the front porch, sipping lemonade as the sun went down. Getting bit to hell by mosquitos and then running inside to make love as the rain rattled our tin roof. In my fantasies, we still lived in that shack back there, even in old age.

"Generally, though. I'm content. Life could always be worse, and I know that from experience." Jason swims closer, and I wade back. "How about you, Savvy? Are you happy? Has time been kind?"

My stomach muscles burn from treading water so long, so I float, letting him openly stare at my half-naked body.

"I am. I found a life I never even thought about. Not that I didn't think was possible, I just truly never imagined there were things like what I have in this world. I'm doing what I love to do as a job, and not many people can say that. I have a good life, I can provide for myself. I have friends, and I've gotten to travel the world."

Neither of us mention love anywhere in those equations, skirting around the issue like kindergarten children refusing to say sorry.

"Well, that's that, then." He nods, paddling away on his back. "We're both happy."

"Yep," I say, feeling the huge void in my life that would make it truly happy.

21

JASON

Hauling my toolbox out of the truck, I go inside to see what Savannah has started working on.

All in all, we've finished the drywall and painting, aside from the bathroom. Half of the flooring in the house still needs to be refinished, and I discovered some loose floorboards in the bedroom that'll have to be replaced. I'll need to get someone out here for the windows and doors, though I could do it myself. There just isn't time with the winery officially opening for the season in just a week.

When I walk in, she's twirling her wet auburn hair up into a bun, and her half-dry shirt still clings to her curves.

I'm still fighting my dick on a mental level, trying to think of dead fish and Rudy naked to get the all the blood in my body to stop flowing south. She was floating in that water in nothing but a cotton tee and some lacy underwear ... what other reaction does she want from me? It's a miracle I didn't grab her in the water and do what we used to do in that lake when no one was watching.

"I need to order the appliances, and I'll have curtains

brought in once you get the windows fixed." She ticks them off on her fingers as if referencing a checklist in her head.

"We've been stalled. Hope that didn't affect your apartment," I say, though we both know it's a complete lie.

She doesn't look at me. "We lost the apartment today."

I try to keep the surprise out of my voice. If they lost it, why is she still here? "I'm ... that sucks."

Savannah snorts. "Please, don't act so sad, Jason. We both know you're not."

Her voice is pure sarcasm, and it makes me smirk. "I never was a good actor."

"No, you weren't. Honestly, though, I'm okay with it. There was too much pressure with that apartment. All of these hoops we had to jump through with the board, the judgmental people who lived in the building ... it was a lot of things."

She hasn't brought up her boyfriend once today, and neither of us has addressed the kiss. We're extremely skilled at avoiding all subjects that could lead to any kind of forgiveness or reconciliation.

"Well, if you want to just finish up painting the bathroom. And I got curtain rods. You can hang those if you know how to use a drill. I'll get on the refinisher machine."

"I know how to use a drill." She rolls her eyes. "My daddy was the one who taught you, after I'd already known how to for two years."

I grin. "Yeah, but I could also get it with one try. You had to measure, level, re-measure, and then drill it so many times, there would be four holes in the wall before you hung a picture."

"Eh, perfection is overrated. It gives the wall some character." She shrugs, looking so cute and natural that I'm transported back in time.

Savannah smiles at me, and I smile back. Here we stand, in the house we bought together, grinning like fools. We might have been kids, might have been insane and spontaneous and naive, but we were really in love. I think that's what everyone, including Savannah, underestimated. Once you fall in love, no matter what age, that never really stopped if it was the one true person you were supposed to be with.

"So then you're staying here a while?" I ask, because if the apartment isn't a top priority, she has nothing to get back to.

"Well, I mean, I guess so? I'm not actively trying to buy anything in New York right now, and I can do my work from here. I'm actually having a nice time seeing my family again, which is a shock. Plus, getting to know the kids. That's the best part."

"They love having you here," I confirm. "Noah can't shut up about it. And I see Adeline at The Whistlestop almost daily, she says Delilah is just mad about you."

Savannah actually blushes. "That girl is a spitfire, I absolutely love it. Yeah, no ... it's been surprisingly nice. I feel like I avoided them for so long because of my own fear ... of what? Now I wonder what I was so afraid of."

"Being around people who knew how much you were hurting, because they hurt that much, too," I answer the question she wasn't really posing.

But instead of getting mad, she just nods. "You're right. I did, I abandoned them. I thought they wouldn't understand how much pain I was in, and then a few years went by and it was just easier. To avoid the head-on conversations, to make up for the guilt and the lost time. Now that I'm here, though, I see it isn't like that."

"You Reeses are a pretty cool bunch." I give her a small smile.

"I had this vision that they'd be cold and standoffish, from me staying away for so long. I forgot what it's like here, to be a friend, to be a family. It's not like in New York, where people are cold and somewhat vicious until you know them for so long that they're only slightly distant. I've missed that you can walk down the street and know everyone's name. I've missed that even if family drives you up a wall, they'll bring over chicken soup when you're sick and peach pie when you're sad. It's easy to forget what community feels like when you're caught up in the rush of the city. I didn't realize how desperately I missed my small town until I was back in it."

It's the most honest and open she's been with me since she came back. I could get into it all, try to broach the subject of her mom and my injury and us. But today has been a good day. We've talked, actually conversed rather than screaming or throwing barbs. I'd rather put on some music, work together in the same space, and cherish the peace for as long as it lasts.

"It missed you, too," I tell her.

We do just that, putting on some old country tunes we listened to in high school, and humming along as we fix up the house we'd never live in together again.

22

JASON

"There have got to be about four hundred people here, man!"

Beau rushes into the stockroom, his face red and his mustache askew. He looks like he's been run over by a Mack truck, which is kind of the equivalent of what we've done today.

"You have to get back out there. Take this crate, it's full of the Malbec that Gina needs." I shove a wooden box at him.

"There are investors here, or at least that's what Nancy told me when she passed by with a tray of bacon wrapped shrimp. She swatted my hand away, but I taste tested, they're fucking awesome."

I scowl. "You're supposed to be serving wine, not eating my food that is for the guests in the first place."

He grunts, the crate almost slipping. "I've been on my feet for six hours straight and serving snobby wino's for about four. I deserve a shrimp here and there."

Chuckling, I relent. "Fine. Now go, we got tipsy customers up there."

Beau rushes off up the stairs, and I finish cataloging the inventory we have here. This is our small stock room, just off the huge tasting room that looks like the inside of the barn. With how much wine the people who bought tickets to Darling June's opening weekend have already drank, we're going to have to make a golf cart drive down to the large stock room on the end of the property.

I can't believe how incredible today is going. It's only the first day—Saturday of the weekend, our doors officially open for the season—and we've had a record turnout. During the pre-order, we sold two hundred twenty-dollar tickets. That got them two drink tickets for eight ounce pours, and one round at our buffet. And that buffet ... man, I was hankering for it. I hadn't stood still all day, but I was hoping to sneak in five minutes to eat. There was homemade gouda macaroni and cheese, ribs that had been dry rubbed and smoked for over twenty hours, special garlic pickles, some of Rudy's pecan coffee cake ... it was a regular Texas feast.

Anyhow, the place was mobbed. Those original two hundred showed up and somehow brought two hundred more with them. Most everyone in the town of Hale was here, along with various people from towns near and far. A couple from California even approached me and told me they'd stumbled upon my winery two years ago and specifically flew here for opening weekend.

Taking just one moment to bask in the glory, I allow myself a raw, fully uncontrolled smile and whoop. No one can hear me down here, and I deserve it. I've worked my tail off these past couple of years, and if this first day means anything, it's that we're going to have a great season.

I am dog-tired, though. Beau is right, we've been at it for hours, and I barely slept last night. It's all worth it, of course, but I could use a glass of wine myself.

Hurrying back upstairs, I'm hit with the noise and merriment of hundreds of people. We have live bands playing every hour on the hour, activities, and face painting if you wanted to bring your little ones, games of corn hole and horseshoes, as well as tables and benches far out in the grass if you want a quieter, more private afternoon.

Guests swarm every corner of the property, from the tasting rooms to the gift shop to the rows of vines, and wherever I go, someone is patting me on the back.

"Jason, this is marvelous!" I turn to see Hope, Noah's long-time girlfriend, approach me.

My heart breaks into a sprint, because if Hope is here, it means other members of her family might be here. Which means that Savannah might be here, and up until this point, she's had no idea that I own what used to be Hale Vineyards.

Hugging her, I discreetly try to look around. "Thanks, Hope. I put a bottle of Pinot Grigio behind your favorite bar just for you."

She swats my arm. "See, that's why I love this place. Not only is it a fabulous escape from my kids, but you memorize everyone's order. Seriously, you've done such an amazing job here."

I made it my business to know all the regular visitor's orders. It made it more personal, and if I've learned anything living in Hale, it's that the more personal you make business, the better it does. Others will disagree, but in my life as a businessman, if the only thing I do is know my customer's on a personal level, I'll die happy.

"Is Noah with you?" I ask, trying not to seem too obvious.

She shakes her head, and whether she suspects something, she doesn't let on. "Nope, just here with some of the girls from the church choir. We're getting too tipsy, have to go make up for it at tomorrow morning's service."

I tip my head. "Tell the priest I say hi. He gives me a pass one day a year, and it's tomorrow."

Hope salutes like some kind of general. "I'm off to find some Pinot."

She skips off, and I make my way through the room, schmoozing and smiling the whole way. Typically, I'm not the most accessible, friendly guy, and the winery has been a good way of bringing me out of my shell. Back in my high school days, when I was the star pitcher of the baseball team, I had an ego as big as the entire state of Texas. After I got injured, I retreated back into myself, feeling less and less confident every day.

Becoming the owner of this vineyard has forced me to use skills and parts of my personality that I hadn't in years. It feels great, even if it's exhausting.

I don't make it to bed until two a.m. But it's with a smile, knowing we have to do it all over again tomorrow.

23

SAVANNAH

"Wow, I'm kind of bummed I missed this for all these years."

I sip my glass of Chardonnay as I survey the vineyard around us, almost with envy. I'd been too young to go to Hale Vineyards when I lived here in my youth, and since I never came back to visit, I haven't gotten to experience the beautiful winery just in my family's backyard.

From what my sisters and brother have told me, the former Hale Vineyards was bought by a long-time resident about four or five years ago, and fixed up to its former glory. When we were little kids, I remember my parents coming out here for date nights, escaping into the serenity of the winery. When we were in high school, we couldn't wait to come of legal drinking age so we could go drink like classy adults at the vineyard. My friends and I had even snuck in here a few times, challenging each other to eat the bitter grapes off the vine thinking they'd make us tipsy.

It only took Adeline about five minutes to drive us here, and she and Lori were giggling and smiling the entire way. They let me in on the secret that they came here about twice a month, leaving either Brad or Noah, both usually, with the kids. They called it "sister day," and that sent a pang of sadness through my gut.

"You're here now," Adeline reassures me, embracing me in a side hug.

We're each on our second glass of wine, the sun shining down on the land only enhancing our buzz on the gorgeous afternoon.

"I think the rosé is my favorite," Lori declares, happy to be away from a nursing baby for a few hours.

She's the drunkest of us all, having not had a drop of alcohol in a long time, and it's hilarious to see. She keeps grabbing two or three appetizers from the trays going around and laughing too loudly at every joke made by people we get into conversation with.

"Rosé isn't even a wine." I scoff, the snob in me coming out.

"Oh, shut up, you bitchy Yankee. If it's made from grapes and gets you drunk, it's wine." She smacks my butt as an endearment.

I shrug, raising an eyebrow. "Actually, I can't argue with that."

"We have got to make our way to the buffet, I'm starving." Adeline rubs her stomach. "Plus, I heard they've got Rudy's pecan coffee cake."

"Why didn't you say so sooner?" I all but sprint up the lawn.

The place is massive, a huge piece of land up past the lake. You can look down onto it, and though others don't know where it is, I can pinpoint my shack of a house through the trees. The vines create the most romantic of sceneries, and whoever fixed this place up when they bought it from the former owners did a bang-up job. It's part farmhouse vibe, part Tuscan villa, and the whole place seems like it's been transported out of a novel you want to get lost in. The wine is some of the best I've ever tasted, and I've been to Napa, and the food is locally sourced plus delicious.

If I'm going to be staying around in Texas for a while, I may just be making several more visits here. I saw the perfect bench to sip coffee and write during the day, if I can declare it my own.

After we finish at the buffet, stuffing ourselves until we almost look like Violet from *Willy Wonka and the Chocolate Factory* and someone just might have to roll us out, we walk the premises. Apparently, Adeline has worked part time here before, during parties and events, and is allowed in some of the off-limits areas.

She shows us the supply room, the big machinery they use to make the wine on property, the wedding suites, and small chapel that was put in last year, and tells us some tidbits about it.

When we get to a big warehouse-looking building on the edge of the property, I'm shocked at some lettering I see at the top of it.

"I'd love to see the stockroom," I say, staring up at the sign.

Darling June. The name sends goose bumps over my skin, but I try to shake them off. Must be a coincidence.

"Go ahead down, owner is down there."

Beau stands there, sweaty and out of breath. I didn't realize he was working here too, and part of me wants to question him. He looks like he's been rolling those massive barrels around all day, and I don't want to bother him. We're not the best of friends, and if he's allowing me to have an inside look, I'm not going to piss him off.

"You go ahead, Savvy, we've already seen it. Plus, I need to get drunky hear some water." Lori is practically hanging onto Adeline for dear life, and I know she's going to sleep well tonight.

I've been a little curious to meet the owner and talk shop, so

I head down. Perry got me into the wine scene, shaping my palette for it over the years we've been together. One of our favorite things to do is head to upstate New York and go winery touring, or on special occasions fly to Italy or Napa. It's extravagant and something only rich people do, but I'm spoiled by it. The whole atmosphere of the wine industry is alluring and romantic, and I've given into it.

When I get to the bottom of the stairs, I only see one sole figure crouching to observe something on one of the bottom shelves.

"Hi there, I'm looking to speak with the owner ..."

The warehouse is musty and ill-lit, but when Jason stands to his full height, I know it can't be anyone else.

He looks just as shocked as I feel. "You're ... uh, you're looking at him."

Now I know why they didn't come down with me, all three of those traitors. Lori, Adeline, and Beau wanted me to find Jason like this, wanted me to discover the secret.

And yet, this entire time, Jason has kept it from me. How easy it would have been for him to brag about this, or wield that kind of power in a small town like Hale in my face.

Then, only one thing exists in my brain.

"You ... you named it after her." I'm so shocked I can barely think.

Jason steps toward me, a dusty bottle of red in his fist. "I named it after both of you. Darling for you, June for her. I figured it was only fitting. I'd be nowhere if it wasn't for your mom. And I never would have bought this place if I wasn't trying to be a better man ... for you."

He bought this winery to prove himself, and he named it after my mother and me. I'm so bombarded with the information I've collected about the winery over the last few hours, and the emotions hitting me all at once. I couldn't reconcile my prior impression of the Jason of today with what I was seeing before me.

My mind is reeling. "But I was gone."

"And I hoped and prayed every day that you'd come back." He shrugs, disregarding the thousands of days I'd stayed away from Hale.

From the way Jason says it, I can tell that relief is coursing through his body. This is the honest truth he's been biting his tongue on for far too long, and now he isn't afraid to say it. Whatever I decide, he's declaring his feelings, and I respect that. When I think back on this later, I'll respect the hell out of him leaving nothing on the table. He wants this, and he's not beating around the bush about it.

"I can't believe you did this. I can't believe you bought this."

I had no idea, in all of my jabs about his employment or insinuating that he was a deadbeat, that Jason had bought this place. That he runs it completely, and so well that it's been featured on TV shows and in magazines.

"You never once corrected me." That thought strikes me hardest.

"What?" He blinks, the heat and tensions growing between us in this dark, cavernous space.

"I said so many things about your job, about you going nowhere. And you just took it. You could have corrected me a dozen times, proved me wrong. But you didn't."

Jason shrugs again, those baby blues boring into me. "The worth of a person is not in what they own or how much money they make. It's about their soul. How kind they are, how they care for the people around them."

He nearly steals all the breath from my lungs. "My mother used to say that."

Those black waves on top of his head shift as he nods. "I

know that. It's because of her that I try to be the kind of man I think she'd be proud of."

And now I'm all but crying. What would my mother see if she looked at my life? Back in New York, I'm tied to a man who values money and power over almost anything. Perry is a good man, but his main goal in life is to amass as much as he possibly can; financially, socially, whatever will further his agenda of rising to the top.

Then here is Jason. A small, humble man from a nowhere town who let me berate him about his life choices without shoving it in my face that I was dead wrong. Because it doesn't matter what he does. This place could go under tomorrow and he'd still be a wonderful person, willing to help his community out in any way possible.

"The Whistlestop ..." It suddenly occurs to me that he's been working there for no reason.

"I help Rudy out since Loretta passed. His arthritis is getting bad and—"

I don't even let him finish. Within seconds, I'm in his arms, kissing his face, his lips, and anything else I can get to. Jason catches me, a wine bottle pressed against my spine, as his tongue meets mine stroke for stroke. We pour everything into this kiss; all the lost time, the pain, the realizations.

How in the world could I have ever given up on this man? I was in such a bad place, so weak and lost, that I judged him for the worst he ever was. If I had stayed, would he have gotten his head on straight two days later and manned up the way I needed him too?

I would never know, because I left. I wasted so many days without him, and deprived us of the true, eternal love we clearly still shared. There was a reason neither of us had settled down, gotten married, or had children.

We were supposed to do that with each other.

My knees buckle and he holds me up, but we begin to slowly sink to the ground. The clink of the bottle rolling somewhere away from us rings in my ears, and the next thing I know, Jason is on top of me. His weight is delicious as he grinds into me, my hands in his hair and his teeth skating down my throat.

Lust, so powerful it nearly blinds me, sucker punches me to the temple. I've never been more aroused in my life, the pleasure of this moment wrapped up in the pure love I feel for this man. His hands find the skin of my waist, and my nails explore under his shirt, up his back. He hisses as he does sinful things to the sensitive spot behind my ear.

I know what we're about to do. I could stop it, I'm a taken woman. But I won't. I'm sick of fighting, of denying something that was heading my way for far longer than I wished to admit.

And just as Jason is about to start undoing the buttons on my dress, there is the sound of metal scraping on concrete.

"Jay?" Beau's voice comes from somewhere up above.

We both stutter, staring at each with drunk passion in our eyes.

"Yeah?" Jason calls out, still on top of me and never taking his eyes off mine.

"There is a drunk and disorderly guest in the tasting room. We need your help."

A weight settles on my chest, a metaphorical one, as the reality of what we could have just done really sinks in.

"I'll be right there," he calls over his shoulder, still pinning me to the floor.

The door shuts, and we're alone in the silence.

"Sav ..." Jason starts, but we both don't know what to say.

"You have to go." I shrug, meaning this both in the way that he has work to do, and we have to stop this before it continues.

"Just ... I don't know." He starts to stand, indecision written all over his face.

I just shrug again, because what are we going to do? He could tell me to wait for him here, but we both know I probably wouldn't. We could talk about this, but how do we put this into words.

So Jason just turns, walking up the cellar stairs and leaving me shivering, everything that just happened playing over on a loop in my mind.

24

SAVANNAH

My phone rings, the tone a different one than a call.

When I pick it up, I see it's Perry, wanting to FaceTime. A knife of hot guilt twists in my gut, because not only have I kissed another man now, but I've nearly let him inside me. I've cheated, physically twice and emotionally so much more than that, and I'm hiding it.

A lie of omission is even worse than a direct one, my mama used to say. You're not lying for any reason other than to protect yourself, and it hurts even worse when it eventually comes to light.

Rolling my shoulders, I paste a smile on, feeling the slime coat my insides. I've kept so many things from so many people that I can barely keep them straight, and it's going to break me soon. Instead of the confident, strong woman I've always believed I am, I feel more like the lost little girl who ran off to New York these days.

My entire world changed the moment I found out that Jason was the owner of the vineyard. That he named it after the two most important women in his life. I was so shocked, still am, about what he's accomplished and how he handled himself as I tore him down time and time again.

Jason's right, that was the measure of a good man. A good *person*. And it's not as if I haven't been half in love with him for almost my entire life. I may have left, may have started a new identity in New York, but I've always been in love with Jason Whitney.

Still, it's easy to admit that to myself. It's easy to see how incredible Jason is, how he's picked himself up in exactly the way I wanted him to before I left all those years ago. It's another thing entirely to act on it. To leave the cushy life I have in New York. To take a chance on the chaotic, turbulent love that Jason and I have.

I'm so unsure about everything, as I pick up the call and see Perry's perfect face appear.

"Hey." I swallow the emotion in my throat, forcing a smile.

"Hi, beautiful," he rumbles, seeming in a much better mood than he was the day we lost the apartment.

"What're you up to?" This easiness between us is what I've craved in our relationship.

As different as the two men in my brain are, I do always know where I stand with Perry. Our relationship, like I've said, is one that is logical. I use my brain to feel things for Perry, which is much easier than feeling with my heart.

"I just got home from the office. It's been a long, long day. I wish you were here to greet me." He settles back on his couch in what I like to call relaxed-Perry-mode.

I notice the gray T-shirt and I'd bet anything that he's in my favorite navy sweatpants. God, he looks edible when he's dressed down. And I love this side of him, one only I get to see.

"Me too." I sigh and really mean it.

Shit, I'm in a worse position than I thought I was.

"Tell me about your day," he says, propping the camera up on what I know are eight-pack abs.

We talk awhile about what we did, all the mundane things

that made up our days. I tell him about writing a scene in the coffee shop, and my mini-date with Lori to go grocery shopping. The boys talked my ear off while we walked up and down the aisle, though Perry doesn't think that part is very funny. He talks to me about trades and stock drama and who bought what expensive car this week.

I listen, trying to get into what normally would be a hot topic of conversation around our dinner table ... but I just can't. And the kids thing is bugging me; the way he brushed the story off with a judgmental raise of his eyebrows.

"Do you want to get married?" I ask, the words tumbling out of my mouth before I know that I'm saying them.

I see the shock twist Perry's handsome, elegant face. "Are you asking me?"

"No." I chuckle quietly. "I just wonder if it's something you see in your future. We've never talked about it."

Perry's phone dips, and I know he's giving himself a minute to think off camera. That pisses me off, his need to conceal emotions before he can give me an answer. Will it be the actual truth?

It comes back up, and the camera is in a different location.

"I've been a bachelor for a very long time, Savannah. I think I've made it clear that I have a strong commitment to you, I'm not sure why there would need to be more than that. Marriage is ... outdated. It doesn't declare how much two people share or what they acquire together. I take care of you, and you take care of me. Isn't that what a commitment is all about?"

What I hear is nothing that has to do with love. You know what I hate that people say? Marriage is just a piece of paper. That's basically what Perry is saying now. And to that, I say, look at my parents who were so in love, they couldn't bear to be away from each other even for a night. I think they only traveled separately once in their entire marriage, and the three days were all but agony, I remember Mama saying.

People who don't actually want to commit say the things Perry is saying about marriage. Because if you truly wanted to make your partner happy, declare things to the world, you'd put a goddamn ring on it so that everyone would know she's yours.

I'm too afraid to ask the kid question, because I'm deathly scared that I already know the answer. If that's his take on marriage, his take on having a baby with me can't be much more romantic. Could I really stay with someone who didn't want to have children?

I feel my blood pressure rising, and all the good will I felt toward Perry on the beginning of this call is quickly disappearing.

Nodding, I know I'm going to lose it or cry, both of which would not be good in this situation. For all that is swirling around in my head right now, I'm not going to make a decision on my relationship over a video phone call. I have more respect for myself and for Perry.

"Hey, I'm getting tired." I fake a yawn.

"All right. You get some rest. I miss you," he says, staring at me for longer than he normally does.

"You too," I say, before quickly hanging up.

God, what the *hell* am I going to do?

25

JASON

The beat of my heart is practically its own techno dance song as I pull up to the house.

I hate that crap music, but the organ in my chest is pumping so rapidly that I have nothing else to relate it, too. I haven't seen Savannah in three days, and I'm going insane.

Our kiss in the wine cellar, interrupted by fucking Beau, was leading to places we'd never come back from. Hell, we weren't going to come back from that kiss. It had changed us, her initiating it, and finding out the secret I hadn't meant to keep from her. Now she knows that I own the vineyard, that I named it after her and her mother, it's all going to be different now.

Or so I hope. I've given her space, but now that we're meeting at our house, I'm putting everything on the line. From the moment she stepped foot back in Hale, I knew I wanted to be with her. Today, I'm going to lay out every single one of my feelings.

When I pull up, she's already there. Her car sits on the gravel, the rented BMW looking worn and dusty from its trips through the Texas rural roads.

My knees are practically shaking as I let myself in.

An Eric Church song hums softly on the radio I've left here since we started fixing up the shack. Savvy's back is to me, her hair tied up in a red bandana, with jean overalls that make her ass look incredible. She's more country right now than I've seen her in years, and it brings me back.

"Hey." The word is packed with emotion.

Savannah turns, her eyes giving me a once-over. I see the blush creep up her cheeks, and then she holds my gaze.

"Hi," she breathes, and the electricity in the room is charged to one hundred percent.

It feels like a magnetic force, each of us stepping toward each other as if our feet won't take us any other way.

"I've wanted to see you every second since I had to leave you in the warehouse." My eyes don't leave hers.

It feels cosmic, this connection between us. We've both finally acknowledged it, and now it can't be turned off.

"Why didn't you tell me about the vineyard?" she begins, all but leaning into me.

Our hands meet, our bodies unable to keep from touching each other. We clasp them, the electric jolt shocking us both.

I shrug. "I told you. It doesn't matter what I do. I learned that lesson the hard way when my baseball career ended. It took you leaving me to realize that a career is not the most important thing in life. How much money you make, the standing it gives you ... that all means shit."

She shakes her head, her eyes glistening. "God, do you know how little of the world thinks that way? Why, Jason? Why did you have to go and crush my heart like that? You're just ... it's too perfect."

This makes me snort. "Savvy, I think we've proved for a very long time that we're far from perfect."

A smile forms on her cherry red lips, but then her expression grows somber. "Why didn't you sell this place, way back when?"

The question makes me sigh, because I've been holding this in for so long.

"I was never a fancy man, Savannah. Shiny things mean nothing to me, if I can mend it then I'll do that instead of buying something new. But for you, I would have tried. I would have given you whatever you wanted, even if I couldn't see past my own shit back then. But you just gave up on us. We were forever, don't you remember we said that to each other? I guess that had an expiration date I wasn't aware of, though."

"My mama had just died, Jason, and you couldn't be there for me. I couldn't ... I couldn't get it past it. Everywhere I looked, I saw her. Nothing would have been the same. So I left."

"I would have wizened up. Shit, Savannah, I was so messed up in my own head. I'm so sorry. I never said that to you, and I should have a long time ago."

She looks away, a tear sliding down her cheek. "How do either of us know what would have happened? You could have stayed in that depression. We could have separated. Losing my mama was torture, Jason. I couldn't be here anymore. I couldn't look anyone in the face, I couldn't reconcile it with myself. My last words to her were so hostile, and I put her through such stress that who knows if I was the one who caused it."

"Don't you dare say that. And you don't know what the outcome would have been between us. Maybe we would have made it." My voice grows quiet, and I look right into her soul. "Did you know I came up there? To New York. I went to bring you home, about a month after you left."

"You did?"

I gulp, nodding. "I spent a night there, and I knew I could never cut it. Those people were sharp and smart, and I never even tracked you down. You'd survived a month there, and I could barely make it twenty-four hours. I knew right then that you had outgrown me. Why do you think I never paid this place off? It wasn't because I didn't have the money. I could have kept up with it, found a way back when I was broke and you'd just left. I couldn't stand coming out here, or even thinking about it. I shoved this house and everything that happened in it so far to the back of my brain, hoping to forget it. I never did, though. For a while there, I thought it would bring you back to me. Then, after so many years passed, I just figured it would fall into disrepair, like my heart."

Savannah walks to the other side of the room, facing away from me. I miss the heat of her hand in mine, and I wish we didn't have to have this conversation.

"I have to go back to New York."

She's just dumped a metaphoric bucket of ice water on me. On my rigid dick, on my beating heart, and on the hopes that were filling up my brain.

"What? Why? No, you don't." I tug on her hand as if it will anchor her here.

"The director of my show, the one I write on, she needs me back for a few episodes. The arc isn't going the way she wants it, and I'm the head writer."

It's as if she's taken the hammer laying somewhere around here and just shattered my heart. If she says this is the reason, I'm sure it's legitimate. But we're just getting somewhere here, just opening up. Savannah has finally acknowledged that she still has the same feelings I've always had for her, and now she's going to leave.

The unfairness of it, the anger ... it gets to me. "And when you go back, you'll see him?"

Savannah rolls her eyes. "This has nothing to do with that. It's my job, my career that I've worked very hard for, thank you very much. I'm reliable and professional in these people's eyes, and I want to remain that way."

"But you'll see him?" Nothing else matters to me as she talks.

Because, of course, she'll see him. He's her boyfriend, after all.

Now Savannah's cheeks grow red, and she rips her hands away, throwing them in the air.

"You want me to tell you that he doesn't even come close? That when I'm with you, it's like a thousand suns beating down upon me? That I can barely contain the urge to launch myself into your arms? Do you want me to tell you that the minute I go back to him, I'll be thinking about what your lips feel like on mine? And how unfair that is, to him? That I've been unfaithful, that I can't think past my own selfishness ..."

She's near hysteria, barely keeping her toes off the line, and I can see it. I want to push her into the madness, to make her fall apart so that I can pick her back up. To make her see that the reason she's so incensed is because she should be with *me*, not him.

But instead of the impassioned, rage-filled response I want to give her, and she's probably expecting, my voice is so quiet that she has to strain to hear it.

"So don't go back. Don't go back to *him*, Savvy. I'm the one you love, it'll only ever be you and me. Don't waste any more of our years with excuses or distractions. I'm yours. Even if you leave, I'll always be yours. Stay and be *mine, darlin'*."

Savannah's shoulders sag, and I hear the sniffles coming from her throat. "This is so difficult ... so difficult. What am I supposed to do, what do you want me to tell you? I cheated on my boyfriend, someone who has protected me and taken care of me in some of the hardest times. And then with us? How can I walk away from you? We're *us*. You want me to say you're the one? You're the one, of course you are. Even after all these years, you're it."

As satisfying as it is to hear her say that, though she left out those three big words, it's also terrifying. Because now that it's all out there, she has the very real ability to crush my fucking heart. It's already broken, already damaged. One more blow and I'd be done for good.

"You're really going back?" My voice is every note of pain and worry I'm feeling.

She doesn't even have the guts to look at me. "I have to. My boss needs me there for shooting."

"But we haven't finished the house." As if that's why she should come back.

"It'll be a few days. I need to get some work done." She shrugs, the words running out.

There is a beat of silence, and so much tension that I want to scream. I miss the days when we could be completely comfortable around each other, though I guess that ship set sail long ago.

"I should go, I have an early flight tomorrow." Her eyes are red, and the confused expression in them wounds me.

"You better come back."

My voice isn't threatening or haughty. It's scared. I know there is a real possibility that I'll lose her once again, for good this time. Or, I might not. She could get back to New York and realize just how much easier it is there. Where there are no ghosts, no lingering loves and sludge she'd have to muck through to repair her relationships in Hale.

The hope I walked in here with has vanished. Now I feel like I'm walking on a tightrope, and at any moment, I could fall into the abyss.

26

SAVANNAH

"Y'all, I have never seen something this fancy."

Adeline swivels around, looking back at me as I sink into my seat. She and Lori have done nothing but talk, extremely loudly, the entire plane ride, and I know our fellow seat mates in first class have not appreciated it.

When I found out that I had to go back to New York for some of the episodes being shot, I decided I'd bring my sisters along. At the beginning of my living in Manhattan, when we were still in contact, I promised they could come out and visit. It had never happened, and this seemed as good a time as any, seeing as I was basically forced back to Manhattan.

Donna was livid when one of the episodes I wrote did not translate to the acting. If I had been there, I could have given input, but they shot hours and hours of crap storylines. And now everyone was pissed. The phone call I got two days after Jason and I kissed at his winery was pretty horrific. Donna was screaming, cursing me out, cursing the actors, threatening to fire people, and definitely threatening my position. My neck was on the chopping block, and even though my personal life was in complete upheaval, I had to put it all on hold.

I've worked really hard for my job, and writing this show is my passion. I can't imagine losing it, especially with all the turmoil in my heart.

"They brought me separate glasses for champagne and orange juice. I've never had one of these not out of a Solo cup!" Lori looks so shocked, you'd think someone just revealed who really shot JFK.

"And these headphones, they just let you keep them!" Adeline's jaw drops.

These two are annoying, but they're cracking me up. Lori has only ever been on one other flight, to see her husband while he was stationed in another country, and that was years ago. Adeline has never flown and has barely been an hour or two outside of Hale.

I'm glad I can involve them in this opportunity. It's not my money, the production company is flying us back, and we all deserve a little first class pampering.

"Check in the seat back pockets, I'm pretty sure they keep chocolate mint cookies in there."

They both dive in, and a few minutes later, the pilot announces our descent into LaGuardia.

The three of us bustle through the terminal, our bags being handled by a production assistant that was sent to fetch us from the airport. I have to report to set in a few hours, and I'll take them with me, but first I thought we'd stop by my apartment.

My apartment, the one I shed blood, sweat, and tears to pay for each month. It's in the West Village, an area of Manhattan I fell in love with about two months into living in the city. I admit, when Perry said he wanted to live on the Upper East Side, I was sad I'd have to leave my favorite area.

But for now, it was still here, sitting empty and waiting for me until I decided to return.

"It's so loud here." Adeline wrinkles her nose as we get into the town car the PA is driving.

"And it stinks. Also, I think that man was peeing on the sidewalk." Lori hooks a thumb back.

I look to where she's pointing and see a homeless man openly urinating in the pickup area lane. "Yeah, that about sums up New York. Welcome to the Big Apple."

On the car ride to my apartment, my sisters' noses are glued to the windows. Adeline is snapping pictures of everything on her cell phone, even if it's a random building that has no meaning to the city.

Smiling, it takes me back to when I first got here. A naive little fawn, hypnotized by everything this city had to offer. It's glamour, it's grit, the heavy air, and high hopes ... I loved every part of it. My heart feels at home here, just as it does in Hale now that I spent time back there.

How does a heart feel complete in two different places, unable to choose the one it should settle in?

"I can see how you got swept up in this." Adeline pats my knee as we pull onto my street.

The familiar line of the trees and the brown stooped steps are like a puzzle piece fitting right into my soul. I love this block, the neighbors and friends I've found here, the peace and chaos both existing at once.

"It's pretty wonderful." I smile, happy to be back in my city.

"I can't believe you lived here all by yourself. Even now, I can't imagine you walking up to your apartment all alone in this big city. But as a kid? You were just a kid. I'm in awe of you." Lori blinks at me.

A part of my ego swells, because no one in my family has ever expressed anything but misery about my move. To hear that my big sister actually thinks I'm inspiring, well, it's heartwarming.

"Thanks." I blush. "Oh, we're here!"

"This looks like something out of a Meg Ryan movie," Lori says as we get out, her eyes flicking up my building.

The walk-up I live in is located in a brownstone-fronted building, with a majestic stoop a la Carrie Bradshaw's. There are paneled windows reaching up six stories, and trees line the street like we're in some 1950-esque Brooklyn movie. This isn't what the majority of New York looks like, but I'll save that tidbit for when my sisters are swept up in the chaos of Times Square.

Right now, I'll savor my little corner of the world, because it is truly beautiful. A tiny piece of serenity in a bustling mecca.

"Wait, you pay how much for this thing?" Adeline asks when we crest the three stories to my apartment, and I unlock the door.

"I know, it's a shoebox." A smile stretches my face.

My sisters are used to wide open spaces, and in reality, you can walk from end to end in six seconds. The window in my bedroom faces an alley, and the toilet has never properly worked. My next-door neighbor likes to play jazz music, badly, at five a.m., and the smell of the garbage trucks that come down the street lingers long after they're gone.

"An arm and a leg, that's what I pay." Not wanting to tell them I pay close to four thousand dollars for this eight-hundred-square-foot apartment with paper-thin walls.

That's the luxury of trying to live alone in New York. It's not that I don't live comfortably on my salary, but staying on top in this city is a grind. One I haven't really missed when I was back in Hale. I love writing, it's my passion. But if I could do that and not worry if my very good salary was covering the lifestyle even a modest New York girl lived, that would be a welcomed relief.

"Well, it's kid free, so it looks heavenly to me." Adeline plops down on the couch.

They only brought a duffel bag each, which they insisted on carrying themselves. I felt like high-maintenance having the PA lug one of my large rolling suitcases up the stairs, but I couldn't carry them both. I huff a breath as I roll them both into my entryway.

"God, the boys have been driving me crazy," Lori agrees, walking around my home as if it's her own.

She walks into my galley kitchen, the cabinets practically touching, and starts opening doors. She comes back with three glasses of water, sets them on the table, and then peruses the artwork on the gallery wall I created behind my TV.

"The other day, Delilah asked me if she could get her belly button pierced. That some other girl in her glass got it done, and I'd be such an uncool mother if I didn't let her." Adeline rolls her eyes.

"She's eleven!" I cry, the whole idea ridiculous.

Lori snorts. "Sounds like something Savvy would have tried to pull over on Mom and Dad."

I clutch my chest. "I would not ... okay, maybe I would."

We all giggle, and Adeline sighs. "Raising a girl is like arguing with a tiny version of yourself. You watch her make every mistake you did, and you can't tell her what the outcome will be because you want her to grow into a good, well-rounded person."

"Teaching lessons, man ... the hardest part of being a parent." Lori nods, sipping her water.

"Well, hopefully, none of your kids will leave the gas burners on after cooking s'mores on the stove and almost blowing the house up." I raise an eyebrow at both of them.

My sisters crack up into a fit of giggles, and Adeline shakes her head. "Oh my God, I completely forgot we did that! Dad was so pissed off, and the fire department had to be at our house for like—"

"Three hours!" Lori is almost wheezing. "Mama just about got the wooden spoon out for that one."

"Those s'mores sure were delicious, though." I chuckle as we wind down from our laughing fit.

"So, what're we doing tonight?" They both blink up at me expectantly.

"Actually, we have a night shoot tonight that my boss, Donna, wants me to be at. I thought we could pick up dinner from my favorite Thai place on the way and have it on set. You guys could meet the actors—"

Adeline jumps off the couch so fast, I don't think she's even breathing. "We're going to *Love General*! Oh my God, what am I going to wear?"

For the next half hour, the two of them rifle through their bags, and we pick out the best outfits for them to wear to set.

After that, I introduce my sisters to Pad Woon Sen and honey puffs, which they devour, and they ask for every single person's autograph on set. Even the microphone boom, who looks so confused that I actually contemplate snapping a picture.

27

SAVANNAH

The next two days are filled with working like a dog, in between showing my sisters the finest of New York City sightseeing.

When I'm not on set or in meetings or revising massive scenes in the scripts, I'm taking Lori and Adeline to the Statue of Liberty, Times Square, the Met, and everything in between. We see *Wicked* on Broadway and they both cry at how beautiful the music is. I take them to their first Yankees game, even though our family are diehard Texas Rangers fans. And we eat. My God, do we eat. I'm pretty sure Lori has had spaghetti and meatballs for every meal, while Adeline asks for a slice of pizza wherever we go. The Italian food in Texas just doesn't measure up, though I do make them eat street meat, milkshakes from Black Tap, and at an Indian buffet that I used to frequent with writer friends of mine.

All in all, it's heartwarming to introduce my sisters to the city that made me who I am today. Hopefully, they can understand why I stayed so long after getting here, and fully realize the need I had to escape the pain I'd left in Hale.

And aside from giving them the grand tour of the Big Apple,

I'm at work. It electrifies me, being back on set. I'd forgotten how alive it makes me feel, to be in the thick of things, watching as the actors play out scenes that I've written. To see stories that I wrote coming to life right in front of my eyes, to be respected for that work—it's what I was meant to do. I'm thankful every day I get to do it, but this week has been exhausting. Donna is pushing me extra hard since I took that time to go to Hale, though I know she's just concerned about ratings and being renewed. She has to worry about that stuff, and I don't envy her job.

Then, of course, I have to introduce my sisters to Perry while we're here. It would be extremely strange if I didn't bring them to meet my boyfriend, the man who has been in my life for four years. If I just brushed off introducing them to the guy I was about to buy a million-dollar apartment with, they would know something was up.

As of now, I don't feel like getting into the details of how messed up my personal life is. They would just want to talk it to death, or sway me in one direction or the other.

We're dressed to the nines as we head for the restaurant, a very upscale steakhouse that Perry likes to frequent. I personally don't think they're food is all that good, but I wasn't going to argue.

When we walk into the restaurant, I spot Perry immediately.

He's sitting at the best table in the house, one he has reserved for us on numerous occasions. His suit is a six-thousand-dollar Armani custom design, I know this because I was there when he bought it. His head is buried in his smart phone, and the waiter is trying to ascertain something from him, but Perry waves him off with a flip of his wrist.

It's a rude and arrogant gesture, and something Mom used to say pops into my head.

"You can tell a lot about a person by how they treat those that wait on and serve them."

My sisters look around, giggling to each other about if they can pick Perry out of a crowd. Part of me doesn't even want to walk them over to him, because my God, he's being a total dick right now.

But then he looks up and spots me, and waves.

"There he is," I say, pasting on a smile.

"Oh, Savvy, I see why you're so into the guy." Adeline elbows me.

It's a short walk to the table, and then they're all shaking hands. Perry comes toward me, his hands grasping my upper arms, and kisses me on the cheek before sitting down.

That's it. That's all I get. The man hasn't seen me for over a month and a half, and he just gave me some European air kiss greeting as if I'm a female coworker of his.

If someone really misses you, they don't care what setting they're in. A reunion of this sort calls for a passionate, all-consuming make-out session, which clearly Perry does not want. He's never cared for public displays of affection, and I guess a long period away is not the exception either.

It's not that Perry is a bad person; in fact, he's a pretty good man. He helped me in a time when I couldn't do so myself and has built me up on a number of occasions. He's taught me a lot about hard work and the ways of the world outside my bubble of small-town Texas. For that, I'll always be appreciative.

But he's also a product of his environment. Perry grew up with money; Christ, his father retired from Perry's current Wall Street firm right after bringing his son in at an executive level. My boyfriend has never had to want for anything; he's gone to the best schools, had everything paid for, and knows all the right people to situate himself wherever he wants to.

That isn't to say he doesn't work hard, because he is one of the hardest workers I've seen. But there is something about coming from nothing, having to pick yourself up by bootstraps that are secondhand and crumbling at a touch, that molds a person into something special.

Perry? He's not it. And it's not until this moment that I realize it. His values, his morals ... they don't match up with mine. I've been leading myself down this path, trying to prove that New York is the place I belong by getting in with some of its most powerful. But one trip back to my hometown, and I see what genuine, determined people look like. Those who barely have enough in their savings account to cover an extra month's mortgage, but would gladly give it away if someone else needed it more. Perry would never do something like that.

And it's at this moment, as my sisters and I take our seats at this table, that I realize my heart isn't pounding. My cheeks aren't flushed, and my lips don't spread wide with excitement. Here is a man that I'm supposed to be in love with, one I haven't seen in months, and my physical response is ...

Nothing. The parts of a woman that should react to seeing the man she's thought about spending her life with couldn't care less.

My mind and heart's reaction to Perry pales in comparison to how I feel each time Jason is simply in the vicinity. He doesn't have to be in the same room as I am, and yet I know he's close. My stomach drops, my heart gallops a million miles an hour, and I can't control my breathing.

When I'm around Jason Whitney, it's like my entire system is short wiring, and that's how it should be ...

When you're in love.

"So you all flew in from which airport in Texas?" Perry tries to start the conversation as we sit down.

Adeline and Lori exchange a look. It's a little thing, my

boyfriend forgetting where we flew from, but it does kind of demonstrate that he either doesn't care or wasn't listening.

"We have an airport in Hale that flies to Houston, where we transferred," Addy supplies, trying to remain polite.

"Have you guys seen New York, yet? I hope Savannah didn't take you somewhere touristy, like Times Square." He scoffs, rolling his eyes.

Lori narrows hers. "Actually, she did, and I thought it was magnificent."

Perry doesn't even have the awareness to look sheepish. I cut in. "We went to that Strand Bookstore stand, and Lori got some cute books for her boys. Then I took them for falafel."

He waves his hand into the middle of us. "I'll take you for the best Mediterranean food if you are sticking around. It's in this underground basement where—"

The waiter comes to our table and interrupts him, asking to take our drink order. Adeline goes first, ordering a glass of white wine, but Perry cuts her off.

"No, disregard that. We'll have a bottle of the Opus for the table." He gives a nod, and the waiter scoots off, knowing not to talk back to the person clearly taking charge here.

It's undeniably rude that he not only cut the rest of us off from ordering drinks, but the fact that he canceled Adeline's white wine for something he thought more superior speaks volumes. The thing is, I let him do this all the time for me. I just assumed he had better taste, and the things he picked were always wonderful.

But they weren't my choices. Which shocks me straight to my core.

Adeline raises an eyebrow discreetly at me, and I know in that instant what I'm going to do after this dinner is over and my sisters go back to my apartment.

28

JASON

My rag wipes down another streak of cleaner, making sure the counter gleams.

As I go, I turn the stools over and stack them atop the tasting bars, the lights low at the end of the night. I'm glad to be alone tonight, to make this place shine before we close it down for our Monday off. The weekend has been a blur of customers, sales and restocking, and I need to sleep for about twelve hours straight.

That is, if my mind allows me to do so.

Savannah has been in New York for three days, and in that time, I've been able to think of nothing else.

Is she with him? Does she miss her old life? Is she planning on staying there? Will I ever even see her again?

Questions like that run rapid fire through my brain at all times, and it's making me unhinged. I'm not a social media guy, but I've even contemplated joining some of the sites to keep up with what she's doing. Then I thought that was creepy, but that's what those platforms are for, right?

In the end, I've just driven myself crazy, and continually talked myself off the ledge. I promised myself I wouldn't call or text her the entire time she was in the city, because she needs to make this decision on her own.

I lost her one time, and it ruined the next decade of my life. I don't want to be that man, the sullen, heartbroken bachelor who lives in his hometown his entire life and dies alone. That sounds melodramatic, but I honestly think about that sometimes. I'm happy with what I have, but I'm not *happy*. Which just shows how important love and the right partner is in a life. Without that, all you have and have worked for is just ... shit.

But I have to have faith in Savannah, too. I've done all I can to show and tell her just how much I want and need her in my life. I can't make someone love me, hard as I try. So the next part is on her.

And I believe, somehow, that the universe is going to bring her back to me. With all that's unfolded the past few months, she has to know that not choosing what we have would only make the both us more miserable.

Looking out over the vineyard, the one I named for her, I send up a prayer. Although I've gone to church every Sunday for almost my entire life, I'm not much of a praying man. To be honest, God never seems to answer mine.

But I send one up now to the big man, hoping he hears it.

And hoping he can whisper in her ear that the place she belongs is in Hale, with me.

29

SAVANNAH

"So, what are you going to tell him?"

Lori leans her chin on her elbow, hijacking the armrest as she looks at me.

I try to use the whir of the plane engine to drown out my thoughts of the last forty-eight hours.

"I don't know. I haven't ... I haven't thought out the details yet."

She's not talking about Perry, she's talking about Jason.

"I'm just glad you kicked that jerk to the curb." Adeline nods in approval, leaning back in her window seat.

We're on our way back to Hale, after Donna cleared me to leave New York again. It wasn't easy getting her blessing to do my job remotely again, but I hadn't worked my ass off on set for the past five days for nothing. She knows I'm trustworthy, and more than that, I'm a great freaking writer. She can't lose me, so she had to agree to a compromise.

I'm free to write from Hale for the next month. After that, I'm expected back in New York. In the next thirty days, I'll have to decide what my future holds.

But something it won't contain? Perry.

"He's not a jerk, don't say that." I sigh, knowing I'll get push back anyway.

"All I'm saying is, if Brad ever dominated the conversation and spoke to my friends like that, I'd smack him. The audacity of that guy, *grr*, it pisses me off just thinking about how many times he cut me off." Adeline shakes her fist.

"He was just raised in a different place than us." I shrug my shoulders, trying to reason with them.

Lori is still staring at me. "And it's made him hard and brash, two things I don't want for my baby sister. You deserve so much better than that. And I'm glad you realize it."

A knot of emotion clogs my throat. "Y'all, I'm still upset about it even if it was the right thing to do."

Adeline reaches across the seats, grasping my hand. "I'm sorry, I'm being an ass. Of course, you're upset, any breakup will do that to you. Even one that was necessary."

"Was it hard? Are you okay? Do you need us to get you chocolate and wine, because I'm pretty sure we can request that in first class?" Lori is about to push her call button for the flight attendant.

I cover her hand. "No! We can save that until we get home."

Their heads both whip right to me when I call Hale home. It makes me smile; the word coming from my mouth. But then I frown, the sadness of what I just did washing over me again.

"Yes, it was hard. I've been with the man for four years, we shared a life together. I'm walking away from all of that, and it's not an easy choice."

"Isn't it, though?" Adeline presses further, being that asshole she said she wasn't trying to be.

Even Lori gives her a look that says *stop it*. "But she kind of has a point. Hasn't it always been Jason?"

"You guys ..." I sigh, knowing they'd go down this path.

"Come on, you can't tell us that something didn't happen

between you two. We were all there at opening weekend of the winery. You two are still head over heels for each other, I could tell that from the pheromones." Adeline wiggles her eyebrows.

Lori goes quiet and then looks at me with the most serious look on her face that I've ever seen.

"I'm going to say this once, so listen good. If you love Jason Whitney, you can't waste any more time not telling him, and not loving him. I know all too well what it's like to love someone and let them go off and do something that might end their life altogether. The man you love, who loves you more than anything, is right there waiting for you. Don't dwell on your ex-boyfriend, who was never right for you anyway, and don't be stupid enough to question your gut. I know you want to, I know you're trying to overanalyze this. Don't. Just go love that man."

Her declaration makes tears well in my eyes.

After that, my sisters just hold my hand and let me rest my head against the seat.

Of course, it wasn't easy. I feel so many conflicting emotions about breaking up with Perry, but the one I don't feel is heartbreak. Which is how I know it was right. What I do feel is sadness for a life that I'll no longer have. We spent a long time together, had the inside jokes that long-term couples do and a routine that was our every day. I feel loss, because he was essentially my best friend for many years. Perry was the one I leaned on. He saved me in a way when I was drowning in New York.

Breaking up with someone that you've shared many intimate moments with is like losing a limb. You've functioned for so long with it, that you're not quite sure what to do when it's gone. I'm not shattered by the breakup.

If anything, I'm relieved. It feels like a weight has been lifted off my shoulders now that I've finally made a choice. Now that I'm not living in a limbo of if I tell Perry about what happened with Jason. And honestly, it's not as if he took the breakup badly.

No, on the contrary, Perry was all but amicable about it. Frowned when I began the speech I'd been going over in my head during dinner with my sisters, listened the whole way through, and then nodded like this was a business deal. Said something about these things happening, and how he was disappointed that we couldn't make it work but we'd be better off.

Better off. He said *better off*.

God, part of me can't believe I'd been with him for so long. The other part wondered what would have happened if we had just moved in together, if my credit cleared and I'd never gone back to Hale.

How strange life is, placing these tiny forks in the road, your decision determining the rest of your life. I close my eyes, but all I'm thinking about is the man I'm flying back to.

The plane touches down, and I'm bolting for town.

Well, not town, but the outskirts of it. I'm not sure why I know he'll be there, but I just do. Call it intuition, a sixth sense, but Jason and I have always shared it and I hope it doesn't fail me now.

I swear, Jenks is going to pull me over for speeding again with how fast I'm whipping around the curves toward number three Covered Wagon Lane.

While Lori and Adeline slept for the last hour of the plane ride, I was lost in my thoughts. And then it hit me. Maybe this was all supposed to happen.

Maybe I was meant to flee to New York, to meet Perry and make a life. And maybe I was also meant to go back to Hale. To see how much I needed to join my two worlds, to see how much I'd lost touch with the humility and good nature of people.

Maybe everything I'd been through was to bring me back to Jason as a more mature, responsible woman. As someone who could work through tough problems and appreciate the inexpressible connection we have.

The reason I felt so much relief when I ended my relationship with Perry was because he was—as terrible as it sounds—a placeholder. My heart has always belonged to the first boy I ever loved. And even though it's insane, even if it might end in us crashing and burning, I want to jump into the fire. *With him.*

My tires kick up gravel, and then I'm in motion, moving toward the house. Wrenching open the door, I hear him drop something in surprise and then turn in a defensive motion.

The moment he sees me, his expression morphs into confusion. "What the hell, Savannah, I thought you were about to attack me—"

"I left him." The words rush out of my mouth, untying the knot in my gut that's been there for far too long.

Jason drops the wrench he was holding. "You ... what?"

"Perry, I ended things. We're not together anymore. I wasn't sure if I could do this ... and this isn't a rebound—"

He doesn't even let me finish. Before I can get my jumbled thoughts out, Jason is picking me up, bringing his mouth down on mine, my legs wrapping around his waist.

My heart all but bursts, exploding into fireworks in my chest. Whereas before, when we kissed, I felt a mixture of guilt and gnawing indecision. Now, I'm free to feel every enormous emotion I've always harbored for Jason Whitney.

He moves us to the floor, our clothes coming off in a flurry of ripping and tearing. The air smells like passion and sex, and the fusion of our mouths is an unbreakable bond. I can't get close enough to him fast enough, and every cell in my body tingles with arousal and purpose.

Jason looks crazed, roaming every inch of my body with his

eyes as if he's trying to put it to memory. I do the same, kissing my lips down his cheeks, neck, chest.

Finally, after what feels like years, we're both free of our clothes, kissing so achingly hard that I can barely breathe.

When he pushes inside me, it's the feeling of being completed. We're two puzzle pieces who have been missing from each other for a very long time. Now that we're back, that we fit, my soul feels at peace.

Jason's eyes blaze into mine, a blue so serene it reminds me of the sea off the coast of Bermuda. We've waited so long for this and there doesn't have to be a preamble. We can have slow and gentle later, but right now, the only thing I crave is seeing him unravel at the same time I do.

"I love you. God, I love you." Jason breathes, moving over me in agonizing strokes.

I don't want it to ever end, but at the same time, his pace is punishing. It pushes me right to the edge while never fully getting me there, and I know Jason is prolonging this.

"Jason ... please ..."

"I could stare at you like this forever." He groans, his eyes all but rolling back.

"Harder ... please ..." I'm wriggling beneath him, desperate for release.

A spark of electricity crackles in his iris, a challenge I've just thrown down. Jason lowers himself, grabbing both of my hands and pinning them to the floor with his above my head. Then he starts to move. Thrusting so hard that I swear the floorboards we redid are going to give out beneath us.

When the wave of my orgasm crests, sweeping me under and drowning me in the tow, I keep my eyes trained on his.

The only pair I ever want to look at me this way again.

And as if he can read my thoughts, Jason murmurs, "forever" before throwing his head back and howling his release.

30

JASON

After we thoroughly undo each other, making love over and over again, I run out to my truck to grab some blankets.

Neither of us feels like leaving this spot at the moment, and I'm not seventeen anymore. I can't lie on a wood floor all night like some romantic teenager.

When I spread the fleece out, I guide Savannah down, pulling her warm, naked flesh against me and snuggling us beneath another layer of blanket.

"Did you ever think we'd be back here, like this?" she whispers, the dark of the night and the hum of the mosquitos the soundtrack to our reconciliation.

"I hoped." I press my lips against her temple. "For a while there, I thought you'd never be able to forgive me."

I don't want to bring the past up right now, but we haven't fully addressed it, well … ever

Savannah is silent for a few beats, scratching her nails up and down my stomach gently.

"The day you got hurt, it was the end of the world. Not just yours, but mine. I knew how much you loved baseball, Jesus, we'd only talked about your making it to starting pitcher of the Rangers for as long as we'd known each other. It wasn't just you that banked a future on your career; I thought I'd be a baseball wife. I thought I'd trail you to games and set up our homes and all the other things that come along with that. Looking back, I was so naive. I'd never ask for you to be hurt, or for your dreams to be ruined, but I'm so grateful I was able to realize my own dreams. Anyway, I panicked when you got hurt. I tried everything to get you up and moving, to make you see the positive. I knew we were in deep, but we could get through anything. We were Savannah and Jason."

She looks up at me, her big hazel eyes full of ghosts from yesteryear.

"But then your mama ..." I say, running my fingers through her hair. "I should have listened better, back then. I should have gotten out of my own shit, seen how it affected you, too."

"We were just kids, Jay. We didn't know how to stop thinking about ourselves, even if we were in love."

It's the first time she's said the words in conjunction to us, even though I said them while I was full seated inside her. I meant every syllable, even if she couldn't say it back right now.

"Still, I should have pushed it aside. After she passed, I was a jackass. I should have never said those things. I'm so sorry, darling." It makes me sick to think about it.

The day of June's funeral, Savannah had burst into our tiny house, screaming at me for missing it. I told her that I didn't have time for her shit, that my dreams had just died. I told her that I didn't care that she'd just had to bury her mother; I didn't even know if I'd be able to walk. I was dramatic and horribly selfish and grieving the loss of June myself. Having two enormous blows to my life within a month of each other, I couldn't handle it. But I should have, for the woman I loved.

Savannah clears her throat, clearly trying not to cry. "We

both have things to be sorry about. I'm not sorry I went to New York, but I am sorry that I left. That I abandoned you."

We have a lot of apologies to make, and a lot of time to make up for. This is a great first step in our journey of healing.

"Are you going to go see her now that you're back?" I ask, knowing that Savannah knows who I'm talking about.

"What is this, take advantage of my open mood?" She smirks, because I'm not shying away from the hard topics now that she's talking.

"I could go with you," I offer, because I've been out to see June plenty of times.

She thinks for a minute and then shakes her head. "No, I think for my first time out there, I want to go alone."

"That's understandable," I agree.

"Gosh, we really know how to have depressing pillow talk." She snuggles into my chest.

I laugh. "Did you want me to sing your praises? Tell you how sexy you are? Because I could do that all night long."

"Learned some moves while I was away, huh?" She wiggles an eyebrow at me.

"I had to learn how to impress you some way." My voice is husky as her hand skates down my thigh.

"Believe me, it was very impressive. But I think I need to see it again," she purrs.

But before her fingers wrap around the place I really want them, Savannah stops and looks up at me.

"What happens now?"

I hedge my bets, weighing whether to admit it all. We've gotten nowhere keeping things from each other, and a decade's worth of words that need to be said are just sitting on my chest.

"Well, I'll tell you what I want to happen. What I've wanted to happen since you drove back into town like a speed demon out of hell. I want to be with you. I know it's not going to be easy, but it wasn't easy back then either. I know you just got out of a long relationship, but this is different than if I were a stranger. Our history eclipses decades, lifetimes. You are it for me, you always have been, Savannah. I've never loved anyone else the way I love you, and I have no intention of letting that or you go again. I want to work on this, even when you cry or yell. I want to fix up this house with you, live in it like we always intended. I want to marry you, and that might freak you out right now, but I don't really care. I want to take our kids here, swim with them in our lake during the summers. That's what happens, at least for me. Say yes, and we won't ever look back."

It's a heavy challenge, throwing all of that on her. I hold my breath, hoping to all that is holy that she doesn't reject me.

Savannah sucks in a breath, her eyes piercing mine. "I won't give up my career, I want to make that clear right now."

A little of my hope falters, but I nod understandingly. "Of course not. We'll figure it all out. Together."

I really mean that.

"It's not going to be easy. I'm ... I'm fresh off of the ending of a very long-term relationship. And you're right, this isn't a rebound, but the sadness is fresh. And the pain of what happened before is still here."

She's quiet for a moment, and I think my heart is about to be thoroughly stomped on.

"But yes, that's what I want to happen now, too."

And then, instead of crumbling into nothing, the organ in my chest soars.

31

JASON

I wake up with my knee and my back screaming at me.

Rolling over, my entire body protests in pain, and Savannah lets out an unhappy groan at being moved. I forgot how much she hated her sleep interrupted; the woman could probably peacefully dream through a symphony orchestra and a war happening simultaneously outside her bedroom window.

"Why did we fall asleep here? I have a perfectly good bed at home," I whine, trying to get my thirty-year-old body off the floor.

Savannah is draped in the blankets from my trunk, and all the skin from her waist up is exposed. She looks golden and gorgeous, and suddenly, I'm remembering why I didn't push more to get out of the shack and back to my house. Being with her last night was the only thing I cared about. Body aches be damned.

"It's nostalgic, don't you think? Spending our first night together in years in the place we last spent a night together?"

"Becoming a professional writer, especially of that sappy

love show, has made you overly poetic. Has anyone told you that?"

"You knew I was a romantic when you met me, not much has changed." She rolls over to glance up at me, where I'm resting my elbows on my knees in a sitting position.

Strands of her rustic red hair drape over her bare breasts, and I'm hard within moments.

"On second thought, maybe we could stay down here a little bit longer." I move over her, fusing my mouth to hers.

But now, she's the one pushing me back. "Uh-uh. I have to pee, and the toilet in there still doesn't work. Also, I'm hungry."

Chuckling, I ease off of her. "Ah, I forgot about the bear that needs sustenance in the morning."

"Breakfast is the most important meal of the day, Jason." She adds an extra bit of Texas twang to my name.

Running a hand across her bare stomach, I give a wolfish grin. "I know it is, which was why I was trying to eat."

Savannah rolls away, standing to her full height, completely nude. "Nope. Not happening. I want breakfast tacos. You owe me breakfast."

I was going to give her a lot more than breakfast, but we could start slow. Now that she was back in Hale, and back in my arms, I was never letting her go again. And no matter how hard she fights me on this, I am going to put a ring on that finger. And soon.

After my bones and muscles allow me to finally get off the floor, we dress, sneaking sly smiles as we do so. Last night was something out of my wildest dreams. Not just the mind-blowing sex, but having Savannah come back to me. I've waited for this moment for a long time and gave up on it ever happening. What we shared last night, and what is still clearly between us today ... I'm not taking that for granted.

"Come on, I'll drive. Where we going, that taco stand out on the freeway?"

Savannah rubs her stomach. "You know it. I haven't had one in too long."

"Remember the time we cut school and went? Your mama almost whipped me, I swear." I crack up.

"But the shrimp tacos were so worth it." She winks at me.

"Yeah, they were."

We hop into my truck, and the memories float around us like ghosts. Only it's different than the first time we were in here. That time, there was so much animosity and uncertainty between us. There is still uncertainty, but now we've committed to working on things.

"Lots of good times in this truck." Savannah sneaks a sly smile at me.

"Yes, yes, there were. There could be some more good times." I scoot toward her, and she presses a hand to my chest.

"I said nope. Food first, sex later." She shakes a finger at me.

Now that I've had a taste, I don't want to do anything else. Savannah is my addiction, and I just fell off the wagon. I need that high now, though I know if I don't get her tacos, she might kick me in the nuts.

"What kind of breakfast taco are you going to get?" I ask her, trying to make conversation that isn't too serious.

Savvy fiddles with the radio in my truck, finally finding a station that's playing an old Shania Twain song. "You really don't remember my order?"

"Of course, I do, I just don't know if it's changed. It's okay if it has, but I'm ... well, I'm trying to get to know this Savvy. I didn't want to assume." My voice is sheepish when I say it.

I feel like she's been holding it against me that I'm not giving her room to be the Savannah Reese who lived in New York for ten years. So I need to make it a point to do so. Just like our talk last night, I'm not going to make her give up that part of herself.

And I'm rewarded with a pleasantly surprised smile. "I appreciate that. But no, I'm getting my same old order."

"So then, two bacon, egg, and cheese breakfast tacos with extra bacon?" I rattle off.

"With queso drizzled all over them." She licks her lips.

"Ugh, queso? On breakfast tacos? It's so ... heavy," I argue.

"Hot spiced cheese? That shit should go on everything." She waves a hand as if her opinion is fact. "Why, what's a better option?"

"Guacamole, duh. Fresh, delicious, avocado is by all means a breakfast category of its own these days. You know all about that avocado toast they live off in New York."

Savannah sticks out her tongue and makes a sour face. "I knew you were going to say that. So gross. I think I'm the only person on the planet who hates guacamole and avocados. It's just green slime that literally tastes like *nothing*. I don't know why you'd want a big slice of that in the middle of your taco."

"As opposed to warm, melted cheese making everything around it just taste like warm, melted cheese? Doesn't sound like breakfast food to me." I fake cringe.

"Then you're not doing breakfast right." She crosses her arms over her chest and smiles smugly.

I glance away from the road and rake my gaze down her body. "I was trying to do breakfast right, but somebody stopped me."

Savannah clucks her tongue, but blushes. "Keep your eyes on the road, horndog. I need some tacos and for you to not kill us because of your blue balls in the process."

That has me laughing, and I forgot how much I missed that saucy mouth when it was on my side instead of hurling actual insults at me.

32

SAVANNAH

Pure chaos plays out in front of my eyes.

Hope and Lori argue over the best way to cut the two roast chickens still sitting in steaming hot pans on the counter. Adeline is trying to corral the children into washing their hands, which has ended up in a water fight in the kitchen. Noah is at the table, spoon-feeding Lori's youngest while making airplane noises, while Brad hauls in another load of ice to the freezer. And I'm trying to set the table without breaking plates while children of all ages and sizes bump into me.

And then there is Jason, who casually sips a beer while I look on wide-eyed.

"This is pandemonium." I chuckle to him as he lays out forks on the napkins I've set next to each plate.

"Wait until dessert. These kids are like vicious dinosaurs." He laughs, nodding at Adeline who confirms with an eye roll.

That's right ... he's a pro at these dinners. He's been to way more than I have; In all, I've only attended one and that was a truncated version with just Adeline's brood. This is the whole shebang, all eight kids, seven adults, and a couple of mangy dogs running around. It's loud and too hot in here, but the food smells amazing and I'm kind of loving the energy flowing through the room.

"You're an expert, huh, Whitney?" I elbow him as we pass on one side of the table.

He tries to grab for me, but I skirt away, not wanting to do that in front of ... well, anyone. Jason notices, raises an eyebrow at me, and then frowns.

"What're you doing?" he asks, not letting it slide.

It's been approximately four days since we slept together ... and have kept sleeping together. If we don't spend the night at my apartment above The Whistlestop, we're at Jason's place. When we're not working, or with my family, we spend pretty much every other waking hour naked in one of our beds. We have a lot of catching up to do, and apparently we're really putting in the work when it comes to the physical side.

"N-Not here, okay?" I squirm, feeling uncomfortable.

I don't want anyone to hear us, even if it's not really an argument.

"I can't kiss you in front of your family? Pretty sure your brother and sisters heard us having sex in your childhood bedroom far more often than they saw us holding hands," he says, and Noah laughs at the other end of the table where he's feeding the baby.

I whip my eyes to the kitchen island, where everyone else is congregating, but that wolf pack is none the wiser to Jason's inappropriate comment.

"Will you be quiet? There are kids around!" I whisper-admonish him.

He rolls his eyes. "I'm not mounting you, darling. I simply wanted to hold your waist. But I guess PDA is something you learned to cut out in New York?"

There is an aggression in his voice that undercuts the easiness of his gaze. Oh, I see. He thinks that I don't want to show off our relationship because ... what? I'm some posh Manhattanite now? That's not really it at all. No, I don't want to kiss and hug in front of my family because, well, I just got out of a four-year relationship. And it feels extremely quick to be jumping into another one, even though we all know the history Jason and I share.

A part of me just feels slutty. I know I shouldn't; I mean, I hadn't even been physical with Perry for over two months before we broke up. But for women, and especially for me, physical intimacy is way more about emotions than it is just the act of sex. To launch into that with another man so closely on the heels of a long-term relationship ending? I just don't want to cheapen anything that Jason and I have.

"No, it's something that ..." I trail off, not wanting to do this in front of people. "Come here."

I grab him by the elbow, pulling him into the hall. The noise of the kitchen dulls to a small roar, and Jason and I are alone.

"I just don't want to rush head over heels into things. I want to be with you. I'm with you every night. We still have a lot to figure out though, and I don't want to make the mistakes we did in the past. Getting into things too fast, being hasty."

Deep down, I am still wrecked by my decision to move in with him as a teenager. It had been impulsive, and I'd lost the last months I could have had with my mama every day.

Jason must see that in my eyes, because he nods, doing nothing but running a hand up my arm. "Okay."

I shake my head, feeling the need to apologize. "I'm sorry, it's just ... it's been a whirlwind couple of weeks."

"Don't worry about it. Let's go have a fun dinner." But I can see in his expression that I've poured cold water on the tiny ember that was burning in his chest.

We walk back into the dining room, which is attached to

Adeline's kitchen, but I feel the mood between us has dampened a bit.

Everyone begins to take their seats as Brad and Adeline bring the food to the table. The kids are set at a card table, their folding or mismatched chairs bunched around it. They're all talking excitedly over one and other, and us seven adults, plus the baby, sit at the big dining table just chuckling at them.

"Remember when life was just that simple?" Noah smiles fondly.

"The other day, Vincent was arguing with a friend about whether mint chocolate chip or cookie dough was a better flavor. You'd think it was a national emergency, the way they were debating." Brad digs in, the table looking like a full Thanksgiving buffet.

Hope divvies up most of the kid's food, dumping plates on the table while the little savages shovel it into their mouths.

Jason sips his beer and then starts serving himself once most everyone has food on their plate. "To be fair, that is a healthy debate. Hope you went with cookie dough, Vince?"

He yells over his shoulder to the kid's table, and Vincent gives him a thumbs-up. "All the way, Jay!"

I saw how my siblings' kids worship Jason in the hour leading up to dinner. He wrestled with them, talked about the local little league teams, and even helped Delilah with her latest boy problem. If that didn't make him the ultimate dreamboat, I'm not sure what did.

Glancing at him, I take in his side profile. Dark scruff marks his cheek, and that strong jawline is one I've been becoming quite familiar with again tics up in a smile at something Noah says. His long lashes kiss his cheeks, and I can see the slightest sliver of that baby blue iris. I don't let my eyes wander too much, because getting hot and bothered at the dinner table would be a bit inappropriate, but I also know what he's packing under the table.

The man is a god, *and* he's good with kids? Honestly, I'm not going to be able to resist him for much longer.

Not that I'm not head over heels in love with him. I think that fact was established the minute I stepped foot back in town. But I haven't told him yet, and I'm not sure how much longer I can keep the words at bay.

"Speaking of ice cream, remember when y'all broke into the freezer in high school and attempted to steal that gallon of Neapolitan?" Hope begins to giggle to herself, pointing at Jason and me.

I have to physically cover my mouth to keep from spitting out my wine. I begin to choke, and Jason just looks at me, hysterically laughing over what's happening now and the memory of then.

"Oh my God, I forgot about that!" Adeline cries. "I think you guys dragged it like three hallways over and began trying to give people spoonful's at their lockers. Principal Magnus was madder than a pissed on chicken!"

"Then it started melting all over the place, didn't someone slip and ruin their entire outfit?" Lori asks.

I finally swallow my wine, gasping for air. "Christy Wright. She had chocolate ice cream all over the back of her cheerleading uniform. It was hilarious."

"We were delinquents, huh? Why did we even do that?" Jason's eyes dance with amusement.

"You dared me to." I shrug. "I don't back down from a dare."

He leans over to me and whispers, "I'll have to keep that in mind."

We discuss some of the memories from the good old days throughout dinner, and the night is one of happiness and family love.

When it's time for dessert, half the room cheers with splendor.

"My wife makes the best pecan pie in the entire world." Brad rubs his stomach, then pulls Adeline in for a sloppy kiss.

They really make a show of it, causing their kids to groan from the other side of the room, and the rest of the cousins to make gagging noises. It's adorable and love fills my chest. I've missed this and didn't even know I had it to miss. I try to push past the sadness that I was absent from these dinners for a long time and focus on the fact that there will be many more to come.

As Adeline sets the pies on the table, and Lori comes in with the pints of ice cream, I slide my hand into Jason's under the table. His fingers lace between mine, and our grips cement.

It's out of sight; no one would know we're showing affection, but it's the thought of it. I'm bending just a bit, showing Jason how much I want to work on this.

How much I want him.

Jason squeezes my hand and gives me a small smile. He knows I'm trying, and right now, that's all we can do.

33

SAVANNAH

When Jason tells me he's taking me on a date, I'm almost too speechless to say yes.

"You know, we've never been on a date before?" I remark as he winds his old truck through dark, moonlit roads.

Jason reaches over, clasping my hand in his. "Hey, you know ... you're right."

"I guess we were always too young to really understand that concept. Now teenage me wishes I played harder to get before I let you touch my boobs." I chuckle.

He shrugs, the headlights cutting past a sign that I can't read. And then the car is climbing up a steep hill, and I have a feeling I know where we're going.

"I promise, I'll make all of those group hangs and seven-person movie dates up to you." His fingers squeeze mine.

When we coast to the top, the big tasting barn comes into view, and my suspicions are confirmed. "You took me to your winery?"

"Don't sound so unimpressed, you have no idea what I have

set up." There is a mischievous twinkle in those blue eyes as he gets out.

Rounding the hood, yelling at me to stay in the car, he makes it to my door as I get my seatbelt off. Jason opens it for me, helping me out as I smooth my floaty white sundress. It's pretty, falling to mid-thigh with cap sleeves, and never the type of thing I'd wear in New York. It makes me feel all of my country roots, and I kind of love it.

"I'll admit, it is beautiful up here. I still can't believe you own this place." Jason takes my hand, leading me to the front of the building.

I glance up at the stars and marvel at the quiet. A couple of months back in Hale, and I'm still not used to how silent the woods are, or how bright the night sky is.

"Me and the hefty loan the bank gave me." Jason winks, and we walk across the darkened tasting room.

"Are we the only ones here?" I ask, glancing around the gigantic place.

"Yep. I told you, no more group hang dates."

Then we're outside again, the balmy night air heating against my skin. I feel utterly alone out here with him, which is kind of a turn on. Why is it that the possibility of having sex somewhere other than a bedroom or inside your house, shower, couch, etc., is more enticing? It's like, if you're in an empty movie theater, there is always some kind of charged sexual tension.

That's when I see them. Dozens of tiny, flickering candles outlining a picnic blanket in the middle of the vines.

"Oh, Jason," I breathe, because it might just be the most romantic sight I've ever seen.

He comes up behind me, hugging my waist, and rests his chin on my shoulder. "You didn't think I'd skimp on our first date, did you?"

"When did you set this all up?" My voice is a whisper.

"I have my ways. Want to go sit down?"

We walk hand in hand over to the blanket where there is a cheese board and, of course, wine laid out. Jason helps me sit, and then picks up a bottle of red, uncorking it, before he sits down.

"Do you want a glass?" He offers me a pour.

"Do you even have to ask?" I hold up the glass that's next to me.

Dark red liquid stains the inside of it, and my mouth practically waters. "How did you decide which blends you wanted to make?"

"What are you, a sommelier?" He smirks.

Shrugging, I sniff the wine in my glass. "I've been to some great wineries in Italy. Napa, too. I've become interested in it. It's still surreal to me that you're a vineyard owner."

Jason pours himself a glass and considers my question. "I did a lot of studying, too. Took courses for about a year before going in to get my loan, and I take continuing ed all the time now. I want to move before the industry does, be up on the latest methods and blends so that I can keep ahead of the curve. I don't just want to succeed financially, I really want this place to be something. A gem in Hale, some place that people come miles just to visit and relax at."

I take my first drink of the wine, and sample some of the cheese and pepper jelly. "Well, whatever you're doing, it's damn good."

We take a break from talking to eat as much charcuterie as our bellies will hold. Jason has picked all the right meats, cheeses and accoutrements to go with the wine, and as we sit between the vines, I think I fall more in love.

"So, this is the best date you've been on, right?" He puffs his chest out.

I tap a finger to my chin, pretending to think. "Hmm, I think it ranks up there."

"He could never do something this romantic." Jason pouts.

I roll my eyes. "What is this, a pissing contest?"

"You were with the guy for a long time."

"And now I'm here with you. I picked you, Jason, that's all you need to know. It's not like I want to know about the women you were with while I was gone."

The thought makes me see red.

"Has he called?" Jason asks, and I know he doesn't want to ask but more needs to know.

I shake my head. "No. He's ... well, to be honest, it was more like ending a business relationship than a romantic one. I shouldn't be saying this to you, but I think that makes me more upset than anything."

And I won't say this to Jason, because it's not proper, but it makes me so angry at myself that I was in a committed relationship with someone who can't even give me a frown as I'm ending things. Perry and I have not talked since that night, nor since I left New York, and I know we won't. Probably ever again. In four years, we had no joint property, no children, not even a toothbrush that was left at his place. When I broke things off, he didn't so much as bat an eyelash, even though I could tell he was upset. I could never respect, or be with a man who didn't at least put up an objection.

"The day I packed my things, you gave me so much hell. You fought for us, even when I couldn't." I remember now, my mind traveling back to that day.

"It was the worst day of my life. Even after my injury, and your mama dying ... knowing you were leaving me was the worst pain I've ever felt. I couldn't do anything to stop it that I didn't already try. I begged, I pleaded. I think I even went into our room and pulled out a ring to get down on one knee."

I played that scene over and over in my mind so many times. Jason hobbling in his full leg boot, trying to rip clothes out of my hand and stuff them back into my drawers. He was irate, upset, and guilt was painted all over his face. The agony in his voice, how he kept repeating, "I love you" over and over again.

It shatters my heart, even now.

But one detail makes a small smile form on my lips. "You pulled out a toe ring, I remember that. You tried to propose to me with a fifty-cent toe ring I got at the flea market."

"Well, it's a good thing you didn't accept it." He presses a kiss to my cheek, sinking down to lie back on his elbows.

There is an awkward silence, because we're talking about marriage and a half-assed proposal, and here we are all these years later. I haven't yet told Jason exactly how I feel, that I'm in love with him still, and that if he asked now ... I'd say yes.

"Let's focus on us," I say, sinking down next to him.

I maneuver the cheese tray off of the blanket and set my wineglass down next to it. "In fact, I don't feel like talking much anymore."

And as I swing my leg over his waist, pulling myself up to straddle him, Jason doesn't look like he's much up for talking either.

34

JASON

The candles twinkle around us as Savannah straddles me, her wild strawberry hair swinging like a curtain over her face.

I push it back, sweeping my palms over her cheeks, and pull her down for a kiss. Our wineglasses are somewhere, possibly spilling into the fabric of the blanket and staining our clothes, but neither of us seem to care too much.

"Would it be cheesy to tell you that this is a fantasy of mine?" I whisper against her lips before invading her mouth with my tongue.

Savannah kisses me back, slowly, lazily, milking the most heated of responses from my cock. I'm rigid beneath her, positioned at the very apex of her thighs. All that keeps us apart is her underwear and my pants, and it seems too thin a barrier. I need it gone, *now*.

"What, tackling a hot girl between your vines?" She chuckles.

Shaking my head, I push my hands under her dress where it's pooled around my hips. My hands find her ass cheeks, and I knead them, causing Savannah to nearly fall against my chest in a wispy moan.

"No, my fantasy has always been to lead you out into the vines alone. Lay you down, make love to you so slowly and erotically that you'd be breathing my name in your lungs forever after. Maybe fall onto some grapes, get you sticky in every place I desired."

She just blinks at me, lust so heavy in her eyes that I think she might maul me.

Pushing the gauzy fabric of her dress up, up, up and over her head, I help her wriggle free as she sits astride me.

"Your body ... it's the most beautiful thing I've ever seen." I breathe, sitting up to bring my lips to the curve of her breast.

Savannah can only groan in frustration, trying to push her nipple up farther so that I suck it between my teeth.

I fan my breath across her skin, inhaling the sweet scent of her, as I work the buttons on my own shirt open. I want to feel her skin to skin. She pushes it off my shoulders, the night air greeting my flesh.

Finally, after teasing her for what feels like an eternity, I sink my teeth into her nipple, laving it with my tongue.

"Jason," she groans, wrapping her arms around my shoulders so as to push my head farther into her breasts.

With her sitting on top of me, it's all I can do to try to wiggle out of my pants. Savannah undoes my belt, all while I kiss every inch of her upper body. We work together to pull each other's clothes off, and when she finally pushes my boxers down, my cock springs free.

"I forgot how much I liked this. I've loved getting reacquainted." Her smile is devilish as she pumps me in her hand, sitting on my thighs.

My head falls back as she works me, cupping my balls while her thumb hits my tip in the exact right way.

And when I feel her hold me still, moving up my body until her hands rest on my chest like she's about to ride me, I stop her.

"Let me warm you up," I beg, not just for her.

I want to taste her so badly, I ache for it. But Savannah shakes her head. "I don't need it. I want you inside me."

Reaching down, testing with a lazy, wandering finger, I tease the hot apex between her thighs. She's soaking wet, and before either of us can say another word, I lift her up, sinking her down onto my throbbing cock.

"Fuck, yes," I breathe, relishing the feeling of her every nerve ending and ripple of wall sinking down onto me.

Savannah cries out, and I realize I've lowered her pretty quickly. "Shit, are you okay, darling?"

"You're just ... so ... big." She shivers, settling down as my cock slips all the way inside her.

A smirk stretches my lips, but I wait until she's tested a few movements out herself to even think about moving.

Then Savannah plants her hands on my chest and begins to rock. And I swear, I almost pass out. The sensations she's causing feel so fucking good, I have to actively think about not coming.

It's my fantasy come true; the one woman I love, riding my cock in the middle of the winery I own, under the stars. I'm a guy, so setting and ambience usually don't play into how enjoyable sex is for me, but I have to admit, this really adds to the moment.

"Jason ..." My name is a plea. "Flip me over."

She wants me to take control, but I don't want to give it. She looks so fucking beautiful up there, and this feels too good.

"No," I grunt, repositioning myself so that I can stroke her harder.

My hips roll every time I'm seated deep, right down to my balls.

With every breath we take together, I feel my heart beat against my rib cage.

"I'm going to come." Savannah moans loudly, and it's the sweetest sentence I've ever heard.

"Oh, Jason, baby ..."

"Yes, darling, yes," I coax her, watching every expression pass through her face.

It's the pure ecstasy at the end of her orgasm, written all over those beautiful features, that gets me. I let go, jutting up into her perky ass and feeling the come burst out of my tip as her cheeks slap against my groin.

I lose my breath, white spots dimming my vision, and allow the pleasure to flow over me. Savannah collapses against my chest, and I hold her tight to me, one hand on the back of her neck.

At the exact moment I'm going to reach for her mouth, her lips come down on mine.

I'm not sure how long we stay connected like that, our bodies as one. But as far as nights in my life go, this one was pretty damn close to perfect.

35

SAVANNAH

Jason Whitney was only the second reason I didn't ever want to return to Hale.

The first? Well, she's sitting right in front of me.

It had taken me almost three months of being back in my hometown to work up the courage to come out to the graveyard, and now that I'm here, I'm practically quaking in my sandals.

Sure, rationally I know there are no such things as ghosts. I'm not sure I'm the type of person who believes in spirits, either. But there is something about being out here, all alone, that makes me feel like I'm facing a firing squad of my mama's judgments.

Not that she had them. Yes, she was disappointed when I moved out, but she never held a grudge against me. These are the fears and worries in my own head, the ones I didn't ever want to deal with.

"Hi, Mama." My voice is shaky as I start.

Her grave is right next to Daddy's, in the middle of the Hale Cemetery. It's a sunny, hot day, and I've brought them both sunflowers that I've placed on top of their headstones. I'm not a newbie when it comes to talking to gravestones, I'd been doing it for years with my father. Mama used to bring us to his grave weekly, make us tell him about our grades, our friends, our sports.

I remember when he died, she was our rock. She lifted us up, didn't allow us to be too sad, and supported our family the best she could. My mother was one hell of a strong woman, and I worry that I broke her in those last few months.

My siblings had all moved out, either with their significant others, some married, or they'd gotten their own places and own jobs. It was just Mama and me left, and she was counting on me to be the one who went to college. I know she thought it, because she said it enough to drive me crazy. I'd gotten into the local college, but had no plans to go. My plan was to follow Jason wherever he went, and school would hinder that. I figured I didn't need a higher education. How stupid I'd been back then.

"I ... I'm sorry it's taken me so long to come see you." Ten years, to be exact. "I hate that this is how we have to talk now. I ... the last conversation we had ..."

She'd screamed at me. Called me a stupid, ignorant girl who was going to get herself pregnant before she was nineteen. Told me that following a man's dream was horseshit, and that I wasn't the daughter she raised if I was throwing away all of my dreams to simply be with Jason. I'd called her a bitch, told her I hated her. Those words burn in my heart to this day, and I've cried many nights thinking about them.

I'd stormed out, taking everything I could carry in my arms and throwing it into Jason's truck. We drove back to our tiny lake house and he held me as I cried. A month later, Jason's career was over and my mother was dead.

"I didn't mean any of it, Mama. You were right, you were so right. I was a fool, and I hope that everything I've done up until now has made you proud. You were the most amazing mother a daughter could ever have, and you must know that Adeline and Lori are following in your footsteps. I wish I could tell you in person how sorry I am, how lost I've felt. But I'm home now ... at least back in Hale. I'm not sure if this is home, if it will be forever. I don't feel grounded. I've never felt grounded anywhere. Well, except with him."

Taking a breath, I touch her headstone, hoping it will make me feel closer to her.

"You were right, all those years ago. I never should have given up my life for his. I've learned that lesson the hard way. But coming back to Jason is the only time I've felt whole in a decade, so I don't know how else to explain it. Now, I have a life, a different world that I think I want to go back to. I'm not sure how to mesh the two. I'm not sure I can leave this family I've just started to become close with again. Your grandchildren would have adored you, Mama."

I wipe the tears from my eyes, taking a hiccupping breath as I sink down into the grass. Maybe I could just sit with her and Daddy awhile, because the words seem to run out.

Not but two seconds later, a bright red cardinal swoops down, perching on Mama's grave right in front of me.

Cardinals are a sign of loved ones who have passed coming down to reassure us they're okay. The red birds have always been associated with a deceased relative or friend coming down to check on you. I used to search for them all over the city; my eyes were always peeled. But it being New York, there weren't many beautiful red Cardinals fluttering down into the smoke and smog of the city.

But here one is, plain as day, staring me in the eyes. The bird doesn't flinch; it doesn't walk around on her headstone or chirp. It just sits there and looks at me for almost a full couple of minutes.

Then it flutters away, a red streak against a bright blue sky.

I look up and the sun twinkles down on me, and a sense of peace washes over me. I have goose bumps, and a gust of air brushes over my shoulder.

It's the closest I've ever felt to the other side, or a spirit, or something that can't be explained. I close my eyes and smile.

"Hi, Mama."

This time when I say it, it feels more solid, more confident and content.

I sit in the grass with my parents as the hours tick by, talking to them about anything that pops into my brain. I know now that I don't have to be scared to come here. Or to talk to them wherever I am.

That cardinal is proof that they're looking down on me.

36

JASON

"So, I'm thinking maybe we could make Pad Thai tonight. I found a recipe online, and I know you're missing it."

My words are fast and jumbled as I set down two maple donuts and coffee next to the stack of papers on Savannah's table.

"Hmm?" She hasn't even heard a word I've said, her head buried in her laptop.

"I said, I know you miss Thai food, and delivering takeout at three a.m. in New York. I found some supplies at the grocery store, and I think we could probably pull it off ourselves tonight—"

"I have to work." She dismisses me with a wave of her hand.

Frowning, I stand, marching over to her side of the table and getting in her face. I plant a kiss on her lips, feeling needy but not caring. I was trying to do something nice, and she's ignoring me.

"Hey, what the!" Savannah pushes me off, and the few patrons inside The Whistlestop glance over at us.

"Good to see you, too, darling." I smirk at her.

"Seriously, Jason, this isn't funny. I have a lot of work today, so I'm staying at my place tonight." Those hazel eyes are both annoyed yet serious.

"Come on, Savvy, you have a couple of hours until—"

"Just because the majority of your work doesn't get done on the weekdays doesn't mean we don't all have jobs. Really important ones." She huffs out a breath.

And that hits me square between the chest. I don't really have a job during the week?

"Well, that's not really accurate. It's just that Wednesdays are my slowest days, and I wanted to come down and pay my girl a visit and maybe buy her a donut. But excuse me if my job just doesn't qualify as important, so I don't know what real success and struggle look like."

I'm acting like a five-year-old, but she could give me two seconds to look up and speak to me like a normal human. Savannah has been working around the clock, and the only time she has a spare minute are weekends, which are my busiest time. I've been bending over backward to close up shop on time during the Saturday and Sunday rushes to book it over to her apartment, but clearly she can't take five seconds for me.

Savannah slams her laptop closed, and Rudy looks over with a frown on his face. "Everything okay?"

"It's fine." She holds up a hand. "I'm just going to work upstairs."

But I'm like a dog with a fly buzzing around its head, I just won't let the annoyance go until it stops fucking with me. So I follow her, stomping up the rickety stairs from Rudy's coffee shop to Savannah's rented apartment.

"What the hell is wrong with you?" I demand, sounding all kinds of needy and jealous.

I know I do, but I can't stop myself.

Her back is turned to me as she angrily shoves the key in the lock and opens her door. "What the hell is wrong with *you*? I need to work, I'm in the middle of a very crucial scene, and you're distracting me."

Following her inside, I cross my arms over my chest. "Is this how you operated in New York? You're a complete workaholic, Savannah! Look at you, I haven't seen you in days, you look like you've lost a couple pounds, and you're short-tempered. I don't know what you think this is, or where you are, but we don't operate like that down here in the South. If a job takes that much out of you, you need to scale it back. Does this make you happy?"

Her expression goes from a scowl to pure, raw anger. Oh shit, I hit the wrong nerve.

"You know, it's been awfully difficult to work out of my normal environment. Without my office or my other writers around. You should appreciate that I've been in Hale, attempting to do my job from here, and not hightailing it back to New York."

Her words feel like a slap. "If it's so difficult to be here, then why don't you go again? It's not like you're not great at leaving."

Savannah stumbles back. "Is that what you really want? Or do you just want me to keep putting you and your career ahead of mine? Because I've been back here for a month, and you haven't said one word about that whole compromise thing you promised."

My mind flashes back to the night in the cabin, when she said she wouldn't give up her life for mine again.

I've given her space, hasn't she seen that? I haven't pledged my love again; I haven't mentioned her moving out of this stuffy apartment and into my home. I've been respectful of her career ... shit, I've been trying to be a better man. And she's throwing it all back in my face.

"If you can't see how understanding I've been, I'm not sure I can show you any other way. I've been compromising, Savannah, yet you've been back to your old ways. Working like the hours in the day don't matter. Ignoring relationships. Slaving away for a career and not bothering to live for happy, simple moments as well."

My voice reaches another noise level, and we're officially yelling at each other.

"Well, maybe it's because you haven't considered for one second what I've given up, choosing to come back here. Nor have you asked if I want to go back! Did you ever think about that, Jason? Ever think about moving away from here to give my career and my life a try? Or is it Hale or bust for you? If I don't move back here permanently, then we're done, is that it?"

"Now wait just one second, no one said anything about—" I try to head this fight off before it gets deeper than it needs to.

"No! You know what? I do want to go back to New York, how about that? I miss it, I miss my life there and my apartment. I miss the bustle and the people everywhere. I miss being on my job in person. So, will you give up everything and go?"

She taps her foot, challenging me. My stomach rolls with nausea, because I had no idea when I picked this battle that I'd be waging a war.

"Savannah, I own a business here, I couldn't just up and leave the winery."

She looks away, emotion clogging her voice. "Right. So once again, it's my place to give up my life for yours."

"Darling, don't—"

"Get out, Jason. Seriously, I don't want to talk to you right now. Just go."

I've already stuck my foot in my mouth, practically shoved it down my throat, so I turn and leave. And hope to God that we can calm down enough to figure this out.

Like I said, I'm not letting her go again.

37

SAVANNAH

Do you know how you know you're in love?

It feels like a fucking semi-truck ran over your heart and body, for that matter.

It's only been two days since Jason and I got into our knock-down-drag-out, the fight where words can't be taken back, and I feel like all of my bones and muscles are just decimated. I've barely been able to get out of bed, drinking tea and writing horribly romantic or gory storylines for *Love General.*

And that's how I know ... I'll only ever love Jason Whitney. I have never felt this way about any other man, not to mention many people. When I broke things off with Perry, I barely even cried.

Now, here I am, slinking around in my robe like a jilted bride or something, watching sappy romantic comedies and eating vanilla chocolate chip by the pint.

I don't want to break first, to give in and call him or go running back. I'm not that woman, and I made my point. It might have been a fight, it might have been heated, but I meant what I said. I'm not going to be the only one giving up things. I came back to Hale, came back for him, because I wanted to make this work as adults.

We're more mature now, we have responsibilities in our life that we have to consider before spontaneous acts of love. I thought that Jason and I would be able to do that, to communicate more, but apparently I was wrong. He's salty and jealous about my work, annoyed that I give all of myself when I'm working on a script. I've been on his territory for the entire time we've had our reunion, and he's mentioned nothing about seeing the world I left behind.

So, we're left in limbo, neither of us wanting to be the one to say "uncle." It's been our biggest challenge, always. We're both stubborn individualists, and this fight is just another version of a hundred fights we've had. We love each other to the moon and back, but we want the other to show just how much they love us. Prove their love.

My phone rings and I jump to answer it, but it's only Cecily.

My family must know about the fight Jason and I got in, because Lori came over here to drop off some spare ground beef she picked up from a local farmer, and caught me red-eyed in the middle of *How to Lose a Guy in Ten Days*. Adeline and Hope texted me no less than twenty minutes later, with lots of question marks and heart emojis included.

I've not really wanted to talk to anyone; it's embarrassing and upsetting, getting into a fight with the man you love, who you haven't told you love, and don't even really know if he is your boyfriend yet or ever will be again.

"Hey, Ceci." I try my best to put a little fake cheer in my voice.

"How you holding up over there?" The concern in her voice is palpable, and I know someone has told her.

"Who let it slip?" I sigh.

"Hope. She had to bring in one of the kids with a rash and

told me what happened. Are you okay? Do you need wine?" Ah, focusing on the important things.

"I've got all the wine I need, and ice cream, too. Honestly, I'm just sad, Ceci. I'm mad, too, but I ... my heart feels like someone put it into a juicer and hit blend on high." I press a hand to my chest.

"Do you think it's worth talking to him?" She pushes, and I know she wants the full story.

I sink down onto the worn couch of the apartment. "No. We got in a fight about New York, about my job and him compromising for me to allow me to do my best work. Or to live a life I want. I'm not sure what it is I want yet, but he hasn't even asked. This is exactly how things went last time, and he was so stubborn that I had to leave to accomplish my own dreams."

"But you love him, right?" she asks.

I haven't said it to anyone yet, but it feels useless trying to deny it still. "Yes. I love him. I'm more in love with Jason Whitney now than I probably was back then."

"Don't sound so miserable about it." Cecily chuckles. "He'll come around. The boy can't be that stupid twice in one lifetime. He's not going to let you go again. I think you both just need some space."

"I hope you're right." I pick a piece of lint off my pajama bottoms, pouting.

"But, Sav?" she asks, and I perk up.

"Yeah?"

"When he does come back to you, be kind. I know you have New York, and your career, but I think being back here taught you that there is more to life. Am I wrong about that?"

I shake my head like a child, not wanting to admit something. "No, you're not."

Cecily makes a satisfied sound. "There are a lot of people who love you here, and we want to see you more than once in the next ten years. I think you and Jason can figure this out. Just make sure I'm in the wedding party."

That has me choking on a laugh. "You always know how to pack a punch and then smooth it over with sugar."

"I'm a southern belle, that's in my job description. All right, honey, I've gotta run. But you call me if you need anything?" A car horn beeps in the background.

"Yeah, I will."

We hang up, and her words echo in my head. Maybe there is a way to figure this all out without anyone having to give up everything.

38

JASON

I stand outside of Savannah's door, taking a quiet, deep breath before I pound my fist into it.

Three days, that's what I needed to calm myself down and see reason. I worked my body and mind to the bone at the vineyard, pored over my books and schedules, and came to a conclusion.

And in that time, my heart felt like someone incinerated it with a blowtorch. I could barely eat or sleep, the colors in my vision seemed dimmer, and I had an attitude with anyone who approached me. I'm transforming back into the surly man I was when Savannah was gone, and I'm not going to allow it to happen for one more second.

My fist connects with the door, and I knock three times. I hear some movement behind the door, and then the lock unlatching.

When she opens it up, Savannah doesn't look surprised to see me.

"Hi," she says, her voice even as she wavers in the doorway.

"Can I come in?" I ask, my eyes trying to convey the apology I'm about to give.

Savannah opens the door wider. “Okay.”

I follow her into the apartment and notice the cartons of takeout and ice cream overflowing in the trash. Guess she’s been handling our fight about as well as I have.

“I’m sorry, Savvy,” I say, leaving it at that.

Her mama once told me that to give a genuine apology, you need to say those words only and let them sit. Don’t follow them up by a bunch of reasoning and excuses, just let the words sit.

She weighs them, searching my face, and then sighs. “I’m sorry, too.”

I give it another moment and then begin. I’ve thought about what I’m going to say, how I’m going to lay it out. I’m not letting her go again, so we’ll have to find our way through this one.

“Since you came back to Hale, I’ve been a different man. I smile more, the world seems brighter, and my heart ... it beats again. In those first few weeks, we were in that tension-filled dance of fixing up the house, but we saw each other almost every day. Then we stepped dangerously close to that line, before you went back to New York, and I saw what could be our future. When you went back, my world darkened. I was a man without a purpose. And then you came back and were fully mine. I wanted every moment with you, whether that was selfish or not. I should have known better. You’re a strong, successful woman, and you learned long ago not to follow your heart before your dreams. I shouldn’t have asked that of you either.”

Savvy looks up, emotion clouding her eyes. “Yes, I did learn that. And it doesn’t mean I don’t want to listen to my heart, but that love also spreads to what I do. I *love* being a writer, and I’m damn good at it. But I also remembered what we had, coming back here. Being with my family ... I couldn’t leave that again.”

She’s still not saying what I need to hear for me to go all in with her, and I lay out the most vulnerable part of myself. This is the part she could shatter.

"I'm not even sure if you love me the way I love you. Even if you didn't, I'd still want this." Though I pray to God. she's still in love with me.

After being with another man, in a relationship I have no idea the seriousness of, I don't know if Savannah still loves me the way she did when she was eighteen. Our blind, all-consuming connection was the center of our worlds. It's still like that for me, but I'm not sure if it is for her.

She crosses the room, turning her back to me. She looks like she's ringing her hands, her shoulders slumping and rising in indecision.

Then my girl turns back to me. "Of course I love you. I've been in love with you for most every day of my life. Even when we were apart, I loved you. Seeing you now, as the generous, caring man you are, I think I love you even more. So, yes, it's the exact same for me. But it still doesn't mean I'd give up everything to be with you. That's not rational, and it's not fair."

So my mind is set.

"I let you go once, I'm not going to do it again. I was too chickenshit to really go after you when you left ten years ago, and I won't make that mistake twice. I'm a man who has something to show for himself now, and I'm in love with you. And for those two reasons, I know that this is going to work. Love might not be enough, but determination is. And mine has strengthened tenfold since you came back to Hale. So I'll work here when the winery is open, and we'll live in New York during the off season. You can have both worlds, no one has to give up anything."

I've been thinking about the compromise for two days. Yes, it will be extremely difficult to leave my business for three to four months in the winter, to leave the town I love and those I volunteer for. But Savannah is more important. If her work and her needs are in New York, then that's where we'll go. We'll split our lives between the states, having family time and my business in Texas, and allowing her to be in the middle of the action in New York.

Savannah looks shocked and skeptical. "Jason, we can't just split our lives. How are we going to do that? And you can't just leave your business, you—"

"We'll make it work." I shrug. "We'll make a plan, talk it out, figure out logistics. We're two smart people, although we've been idiots for the past ten years, staying away from each other. Let's not do that again. We have a home here, my home. You have an apartment. I'll run the winery remotely during the winter, it doesn't take that much upkeep during those months and I have some people who will help out. We've already proved you can work remotely, although you drive yourself insane. And who knows where either of us will be tomorrow? We could both be out of jobs, crazier things have happened. The only thing I know is that I want to be next to *you* wherever we are."

A laugh bubbles up out of her throat, and I walk toward her. "What's so funny?"

"This." She points between us. "This is insane. We're insane."

"Yes, we are. But haven't we always been? Now, get over here and tell me you love me about a thousand more times."

They're the last words either of us says before I grab her and haul her to the creaky Whistlestop apartment bed.

39

SAVANNAH

"Are you sure you're okay?"

I look over at Jason, who is still a little pale.

He nods. "Just a little bit shaky still from that landing, but I'll be okay."

A smile stretches my cheeks as I pat his hand. "You'll get used to the flying, it'll be second hand by this winter."

Lacing his fingers in mine, he takes a deep breath. God damn, he's cute. I find it adorably sweet that the man who is literally the size of a hulking tree branch and can fling me across a mattress easily gets queasy on an airplane.

We're in a taxi, on our way to my apartment. Well, on our way into the city from LaGuardia. I know we have to drop our bags at the apartment, but I want to show Jason something first, really introduce him to the city that will be his home half the time.

It's been about two weeks since we decided to compromise with his solution of spending half the year in Texas, and half the year here. At first, I thought he was crazy, and that it would never work. But a couple of sit-down, deep-talk planning sessions later and we've got the best plan we could think up.

From October to the beginning of March, we'll live in New York. It works out kind of perfectly because my shooting schedule for *Love General* starts in October and ends in January, with a March premiere date. We'll be packing up to go back to the country just as a new season premieres, and I'll be able to get a good couple months of remote writing in.

So then, from March to September, we'll be back in Hale. Jason can run the vineyard and tend to all the events and parties they have slated. I can work from his house, where we'll live, and spend time with my family. During those winter months, I've already made my brother and sisters promise to make a trip to New York, and I'm sure we'll fly back to Hale more than once.

It's the best of both worlds, or at least it seems like it. We haven't gotten through an entire test year yet. Hell, it hasn't even begun, but I think this will be the compromise we both need. We love each other; we love our worlds, and now we'll combine them.

I suggested taking a short three-day trip here so Jason could really see what New York is like. I plan to take him to the touristy spots, but more than that, I'm going to show him the spots I love. I'll also take him to work, to show him just exactly what it is that I do.

It'll be his introduction to the city, and I pray that he loves it. I hope he falls in love with this chaotic, jumbled mess as much as I did when I showed up here as an eighteen-year-old.

We pull up to the Freedom Tower, and Alana waits out front for us.

"Hey, Savannah, how you doing? Long time no see." She gives me an air kiss and then waits for me to introduce Jason.

"Alana, so good to see you, thanks for doing this. This is Jason." Calling him my boyfriend seems silly.

Probably because I'm almost thirty, but also because we are so much more than that. After admitting that I love him, we've been stronger than ever. We also haven't been able to keep our hands off each other, which proved difficult on the airplane as he was trying to frisk me while almost barfing into the seat-back nausea bag.

"Nice to meet you. All right, come on up. We held the time just for you."

Jason glances at me, because I haven't told him what we're doing, and I smile sneakily. This is one of the coolest activities in New York, in my opinion, out of all the tourist traps. And you usually have to wait in a long line or go up with twelve other people who crowd you and such. But not today. No, when Donna, my boss, knows the marketing manager for the Freedom Tower, she pulls some strings to get you a private elevator ride up to the observatory.

"What're you up too?" Jason leans over, whispering in my ear.

My hand laces through his, and I press up to give him a kiss on the cheek. "Trying to make you fall in love."

"With you? Impossible. Already happened a long time ago."

I blush. "No, not with me. With the city."

We walk inside the enormous glass structure, and Jason marvels. "Wow, this place is ..."

"Spectacular, right?" I say as we bypass the line of ticket holders.

I feel slightly guilty as we do so, but I need to make this point so that Jason can see he's not making a mistake choosing this to be with me. I keep feeling guilty, like he'll hate it here eventually, so I need to do everything in my power to show him otherwise.

"Hmm, got connections, huh?" he says, noticing as we step into the elevator.

"Maybe." I shrug, and Alana presses the buttons. "Okay, watch this."

Jason and I press our noses to the glass as it rises, one of the fastest elevators in the entire world. It's a glass box, showing us the entire borough of Manhattan as we rise up over it. It's less than a minute, but I hear his intake of breath, the wonder going through his mind and emotions. It's the same way I felt the first time I took this ride.

The elevator dings, and now we're at the top. I keep my hand in Jason's as we walk over to the wall of glass windows in the observatory. It's a room made of windows, with views looking out to the entire city.

"This is incredible." His voice is reverent as we look out the windows.

I agree. "It's one of my favorite views and gives you a bird's eye of exactly how big this place is. When you're walking down on the street, it's easy to feel small. To feel like the whole world is going to consume you. But when I come up here, I feel like I can conquer it."

I move into his arms, so that I can wrap mine around his waist. "I hope you can learn to love it here, too. Thank you, Jason, for making this sacrifice. I know it wasn't an easy one, and I think this will be incredible for both of us."

He looks down at me with those beautiful blue orbs. "Now I just have to find some places to volunteer."

"I don't think you'll have any trouble with that here. Actually, I think a lot of places are in dire need of someone like you." I lean my head on his chest.

"All right, New York. I think I'm ready for you." He rests his chin on the top of my scalp.

And I'm ready for the rest of my life with him.

40

JASON

It feels strange, being back in Hale after the intensity of New York City.

As much as I wasn't looking forward to the trip, I have to admit, I enjoyed it. I've never lived anywhere else but Hale, and although I proposed the compromise, I was on edge. New York is a big change, and I'm still trying to figure out what I'll do or how I'll fit in the city.

With Savannah's help and connections, I can definitely find some charities or shelters to help out at while she works, which would mean a lot to me. And I'll be busy with off-season remote work on the winery, since we're only expanding more each year.

But I really did enjoy myself. She showed me all of her favorite places, places I can imagine us going while we live there in the winter. It's a different pace of life, but there is something exciting about it, and something that internally motivates you. You can't be lazy or unsuccessful in that city, that's what it feels like.

I'm glad to be back in our hometown, though. The buzzing of noise in my head is replaced by the chirp of birds and the hum of mosquitos. I'm happy to see all the familiar faces and get back to my house with its backyard and quiet street.

Today, I asked Savannah to meet me out at the house. Our house. The thing that brought us back together.

I have a gold-plated number I bought to hang right next to the front door, a finishing touch. That number three is the last thing we need to add to the house to make it ready to sell. Together, we paid off the back taxes and mortgage last week, so as far as financials go, we're in a place to sell it.

Although, I'm not sure that's what I want to do now.

I hear her car crunch on the driveway as she pulls up, and a couple seconds later she's floating through the door. God, she's gorgeous. I fell in love with a wild, beautiful girl and she's transformed into an even more beautiful woman.

"Wow, this place looks amazing. I can't believe we did this." She looks around at our work.

"I kind of can't either. Or at least, I can't believe you did manual labor. You really wanted to get out of Hale that badly," I tease her.

She rolls her eyes. "At the beginning, yes. I was excited for my apartment in New York. But now, I'm excited for both."

We've talked about getting a bigger place in the same neighborhood she lives in in Manhattan. I actually really like the West Village, it has a little bit of that Hale feel in the middle of the city.

"I thought we could add the number to the door. Together." I hold up the gold three.

"Oh, let's!" She claps her hands and goes out front.

Savannah insisted on painting the front door a bright red, and I have to admit it brings out the cabin. The shingled siding is a dark gray, and with the red door and yellow shutters, the house looks like something out of a storybook.

Together, we nail the number next to the door, and I polish it with a rag.

"So, do we sell or keep it?" she asks, glancing at our hard work as we stand on the front porch.

"Well, that depends. I thought if we kept it, we could save it for the future. It is by the lake, a prime spot for summer swimming. Maybe we could put a few bunk beds on that side of the room, for visitors. Or kids ..."

"Oh yeah, and what does that depend on?" Savannah gives me a sly grin.

"On if you marry me," I tell her, pulling her into me.

"I thought we already agreed on that. Did I not tell you that?" She taps her chin with a taunting expression on her face.

"No, you didn't. Because I didn't ask." I pull the ring from my back pocket, holding it out to her. "But I am now."

Savannah's face is pure shock as I bend down on one knee. "Darling, my one and only darling, will you marry me? Spend forever as my partner, my only love?"

She begins to cry, nodding her head vehemently. But yes isn't the word that pops out of her mouth.

"It isn't a toe ring," she garbles through a laugh and tears.

I crack up, hanging my head and then looking back up at her. "No, I'm older and wiser, remember?"

"Yes. And yes, of course, I'll marry you."

She bends as I stand, our bodies meeting in the middle. I engulf her in a hug, and at some point, our lips find each other. We get lost in the moment, our kisses heating up, and pretty soon, I'm grinding against her.

"We should probably put this ring on you before I don't have control left." I break off, laughing.

Picking up her left hand, I slide the diamond onto her ring finger. It sparkles, and she sucks in a breath.

"Jason, it's perfect."

I wipe some fake sweat off my brow. "Good, because your sisters and Cecily went back and forth so many times, I thought I'd end up with a lump of coal from the jewelers."

She throws her head back laughing. "Oh my God, I can't believe we're going to get married."

"Wasn't this the plan all along?" I kiss her forehead.

"Yes, there were just some obstacles and challenges along the way. I'm marrying the first man I ever kissed."

"And I'll be the last."

I say that with happiness, with satisfaction.

Deep down, I always knew I'd marry Savannah Reese. It just took a lot longer than I anticipated. Which will only make me appreciate the years we have now, to make our life together.

EPILOGUE

SAVANNAH

One Year Later

We make plans, and the universe laughs.

When Jason and I made a plan to live half our year in New York, and the other half in Hale, we didn't anticipate trying to plan a wedding while doing so. Or at least, I didn't, since he was the one who proposed and knew he was planning to.

It's difficult enough to coordinate a wedding venue and all the things that come with that checklist while you're hundreds of miles away. But what's even harder?

Finding out you're pregnant five months before your wedding and already having deposits down on everything.

"I feel enormous," I whine as Jason puts his arms around me. "You can barely dance with me."

My husband—*oh my God, he's my husband* rolls his eyes.

"You barely have a bump, and you look incredible." Jason bends to me, whispering in my ear. "You smell amazing, your skin feels amazing. You're sure we have to stay here for the entire reception. I have *a lot* of things to show you back in that bridal suite."

I chuckle as he nuzzles my neck. "I can't drink at my wedding, the cake hasn't arrived yet, and I spent months planning this thing. You bet your ass we're staying."

"Fine. But I'd rather look at your ass." He winks.

In reality, I'm just being a brat. I know I barely have a bump, and I still got to wear my dream dress. It's an A-line lace dress with invisible lace long sleeves and a dramatic cut in the back, almost down to my tailbone. My favorite designer in New York helped me collaborate on it, and I'm more in love with this dress than about ninety-five percent of this wedding.

It's been a wonderful day, but I kind of wish we did something smaller. Practically the entire town of Hale is here, and I'm already tired. It's only an hour into the wedding, and I'd like a foot rub and some cookies in the tub in our suite.

I guess that's what happens when you get knocked up accidentally before your wedding.

Not that I'm complaining. I think it's just that Jason and I are so much more excited for the baby than we are about being married. We agreed that we could go down to city hall, but I think everyone else was so excited that we just went ahead with the wedding.

What we're ecstatic about is the birth of our child in four months. The pregnancy didn't happen on purpose, but when we found out, after I peed on a stick in our New York apartment, we both cried happy tears for hours. It feels like the thing we were meant for, and the thing that was meant for us.

Jason is so happy, he's been reading baby books for months and going on and on about building a crib. He's going to be the most incredible father to our daughter.

That's right, we're having a little baby girl. And for the name, we're thinking June.

Adeline and Brad shuffle dance over to us, bumping their hips with ours.

"Hi, newlyweds," my sister singsongs.

"Heyyy." I wiggle my fingers at her. Okay, so being the bride and groom isn't all bad. This is actually pretty fun, and you can feel all the love in the room.

My family is ecstatic that not only are we back in Hale for a few months, but that we're finally man and wife. They've been really helpful with everything and helping me get ready for the baby.

"What're you going to do, cart a baby from the coast to the middle of the US every six months? That's not fair, I need baby snuggles," Adeline whines.

I bop her on the nose, giving her an admonishing look. "Oh Addy, none of that today. This is my wedding, and that means no one has to think about anything regarding logistics or setting down roots. We'll figure it out when the time comes, in the way that's best for us."

That's the only thing I haven't missed, the grief. They want us to stay put in Hale with the baby for good, but I still have to work. I have no intention of giving up work, though I'll stay home for a few months. We'll figure it out ourselves, now that we've mastered the first year of dual-city living.

The last year has been better than either of us expected, I think. The compromise works pretty much to perfection. Being in New York for shooting has been amazing, it's much better to be in the environment, and I feel like my writing is on another level. At least by measurement of the ratings for last season killing it.

And Jason has been helping out two local women's shelters, teaching the kids sports and serving meals. He's there most days, and it's become his passion project. He talks about the kids all the time, and we even set up a meet and greet for some of the mothers and the actors on *Love General*.

When he's not there, he's working on the winery, which had its best year ever last summer. Now we're back for the beginning of the season, and it's looking like it'll be a banner year for Darling June Vineyards.

The song switches from a slow one to a fast one, and Jason whispers in my ear, "I just saw them wheel the cake in, want to go cut into it while no one is looking?"

I bite his ear in a spot that makes him shiver. "You still know how to make me wild."

Hand in hand, the boy I've always loved leads me to our wedding cake.

And we dig in, not caring what the rest of the world is doing.

Do you want your **FREE** Carrie Aarons eBook?

All you have to do is **sign up for my newsletter**, and you'll immediately receive your free book!

ALSO BY CARRIE AARONS

Standalones:

Love at First Fight

Nerdy Little Secret

That's the Way I Loved You

Fool Me Twice

Hometown Heartless

The Tenth Girl

You're the One I Don't Want

Privileged

Elite

Red Card

Down We'll Come, Baby

As Long As You Hate Me

All the Frogs in Manhattan

Save the Date

Melt

When Stars Burn Out

Ghost in His Eyes

On Thin Ice

Kissed by Reality

The Callahan Family Series:

Warning Track

The Rogue Academy Series:

The Second Coming

The Lion Heart

The Mighty Anchor

The Nash Brothers Series:

Fleeting

Forgiven

Flutter

Falter

The Flipped Series:

Blind Landing

Grasping Air

The Captive Heart Duet:

Lost

Found

The Over the Fence Series:

Pitching to Win

Hitting to Win

Catching to Win

Box Sets:

The Complete Captive Heart Duet

The Over the Fence Box Set

ABOUT THE AUTHOR

Author of romance novels such as The Tenth Girl and Privileged, Carrie Aarons writes books that are just as swoon-worthy as they are sarcastic. A former journalist, she prefers the love stories of her imagination, and the athleisure dress code, much better.

When she isn't writing, Carrie is busy binging reality TV, having a love/hate relationship with cardio, and trying not to burn dinner. She's a Jersey girl living in Texas with her husband, daughter, son and Great Dane/Lab rescue.

Please join her readers group, Carrie's Charmers, to get the latest on new books, as well as talk about reality TV, wine and home decor.

You can also find Carrie at these places:

Website

Facebook

Instagram

Twitter

Amazon

Goodreads

Made in the USA
Coppell, TX
17 January 2021

48343742R00135